NEVER ALONE

Ellen
Jorgey

Happy
Reading

NEVER ALONE

Ellen Jorgy

www.ellenjorgy.com

Facebook @ellenjorg2

ISBN   978-0-9953035-3-9

Never Alone

To keep her he had to remember, but if he remembered, he could lose her forever…

A Note To Readers

This book contains kissing (GASP!)

It has always been a disappointment to me that Inspirational Romance is often written with little or no passion between the protagonists. I don't know anyone, Christians included, who didn't have passionate thoughts and feelings about the person they fell in love with, even if their behavior was exemplary. To write without passion is, I think, unrealistic and not enjoyable to read.

Some characters in this story are not Christian, so they don't behave and speak like Christians. Would you expect them to?

Some characters in this story hear God speak to them. No, not out loud, but in their head or heart as you wish. Perhaps you have not experienced this for yourself, but I have, though not very often. Anything like that, portrayed in this story, has been experienced by myself or someone I know directly. Please don't tell me "God can't/won't/doesn't…" because He has!

If you believe Christians cannot, or should not, experience passionate thoughts and feelings, or make mistakes, then perhaps this book is not for you.

As for everyone else, hang on for the ride! I hope you have as much fun reading as I did writing.

Blessings,

Ellen

Chapter One

Amy Scott peered at the two beams of light from her kitchen window as the knot of anxiety in her belly tightened another notch. It's nothing, she told herself. You're just being paranoid. She kept watching the unmoving lights. Something was wrong. She could feel it.

She had been watching the headlights as she washed up her dishes. The sun had already sunk behind the mountains, leaving the peaks looming as black silhouettes in a twilight sky. Across the valley, two white beams wound their way along the road, winking on and off as they passed behind thick bands of trees only to reappear moments later, a little farther along.

She'd turned away, lost in thought about her life, or lack thereof, wishing for someone to come along and ease some of the loneliness. Keep busy. Wipe down the table. Sweep up the dog hair. Don't think too much. When she'd turned back, the headlights were still visible, but had stopped moving.

And there they remained.

"Why stop there?" she muttered to herself. Why even be there in the first place?

That road accessed a few summer cabins, and hikers used it to get to the trail heads, but at this time of day in late September they should be coming back, not heading up. She studied the headlights a bit longer. Something was definitely off. It took her a few moments to realize the lights were at an odd angle, almost as if they were pointing down the mountainside.

"It's *nothing,*" she told herself. "Just some kids stopped to look at the moon and make out."

But there was no moon. The knot of tension in her belly grew with each passing moment. What if there'd been an accident?

With a sigh of exasperation at her own wild imagination, Amy grabbed her work jacket with the words "Scott Veterinary Services" embroidered across the back, snatched her keys off the hook, and strode out the kitchen door into the parking lot. She'd have no peace at all tonight if she didn't just go check it out. She'd just drive by. Prove to herself all was well. No one would have to know what a twit she was being.

A chill wind whipped at her long blonde hair and chased a few dry leaves across the gravel as Amy stepped out into the parking lot. She briefly considered taking her Golden Retriever, Bella, along for the ride, but dismissed the idea. She'd only be gone a few minutes anyway.

Amy started up her old truck and turned left out of her parking lot onto the highway that headed into town. A few hundred yards later she turned right onto the smaller road heading towards the far side of the valley and up the mountainside. She kept her eyes peeled for wildlife and the offending headlights, but the road was so twisting that she couldn't see too far ahead. As she strained to see around each new curve in the road, the minutes dragged by with nothing more on the roadside than the trees and an occasional signpost.

"This is dumb," she said to herself. The car had obviously moved on and here she was still driving around like an idiot. Now if she could just find a safe spot to turn around...

Amy rounded one last bend. Her blood turned cold as the headlights suddenly appeared in front of her. Braking hard, she pulled off onto the gravel shoulder and sat there, staring at the scene in front of her, struggling just to breathe.

She'd been right about the lights appearing to point down the mountain. The black sports car was off the road, half hanging down the edge of the escarpment. This was her worst nightmare come back to haunt her.

Several large pine trees stood like silent sentinels, guarding the cliffside, and held the car in place. On either side of them, the edge dropped off sharply, several hundred feet down. It was a miracle the car hadn't gone right down the mountain.

Amy sat in her truck, momentarily paralyzed, her fingers strangling the steering wheel, and her heart racing. White steam poured from the front of the stricken car, but she was no longer seeing the present.

Once again, she was trapped in her own car, so many years ago, screaming for help, bloody hands pounding on the window, choking on antifreeze steam. The pain had been excruciating. She was trapped, unable to move, thinking the car was on fire.

The old panic swelled anew as it threatened to swallow her whole all over again.

Amy clenched her eyes tightly shut to block out the sight for a moment. Forcing herself to breathe slowly and deeply she whispered, "God help me! I don't know what to do!"

Almost instantly, as if an unseen hand were pouring cold water on her, Amy felt a coolness run from her head, down through the core of her body and out through her limbs. The panic eased; and a calmness, impossible only moments before, took over. She blinked slowly and looked around. Taking a shaky breath, she reached for her phone. Her hand skimmed the empty passenger seat. No phone.

Amy frantically patted down her jacket pockets. No telltale bulge. Shoot! She must have left it at home. Now what?

The panic reasserted itself, taking over again, but she fought it down. God was with her, she reminded herself. He was helping her. She'd get through this somehow.

"Okay, Lord, now what?"

Amy knew, deep in her gut, she couldn't just drive away to summon help. Help would have to come from her. Now.

Taking a deep breath to calm herself, Amy slid out of her truck and approached the car cautiously. Stepping with care, she inched towards the precipice and evaluated the situation. The car had spun 180 degrees and slammed the driver's side into the trees where it remained, wedged against them. On closer inspection, the trees themselves leaned precariously outward, the impact of the car having loosened their root systems from the embankment.

A movement within the car caught her attention. She heard the door handle rattle as the car shifted ominously. The trees creaked as they rubbed against the metal and a shower of dirt and pebbles cascaded down the cliff, the noise of them bouncing off each other seeming to go on forever. Amy hesitated, holding her breath, watching. Would the trees hold? The door opened a fraction, but then nothing. Amy watched a moment more, but all remained silent.

Pushing her fear down deeper, Amy inched up to the car and carefully opened the door. Inside a man lay sprawled across both seats with his hips still on the driver's side. She guessed he had been trying to drag himself over to the passenger side because he lay face down with his arms extended towards the door, covered in small translucent orbs of shattered glass. All that Amy could tell about him, in the evening gloom, was that he was broad-shouldered with very dark hair. She also knew from his odd angle, that his seat belt was still done up. He was trapped.

Amy stood, staring into the car, struggling within herself, shaking like a leaf. She didn't dare get into that car for fear it would slide off the cliff with them both inside. She couldn't just leave him trapped there while she drove off to get help. What if the car fell before she got back? She had no phone. She couldn't go in there, but she couldn't just do nothing, not after what she'd been through herself. Amy closed her eyes, whispered "God help me," and made her decision.

Using her own memories now as a source of strength, Amy knelt down in the doorway and spoke gently but firmly. "My name is Amy. I'm here to help you."

He lifted his head to look at her, his eyes dazed and unfocused. She noticed a dark wet mark down the left side of his face and guessed it must be blood.

"You need to unbuckle your seat belt," she instructed firmly, her voice shaking in spite of her best efforts to stay calm.

The man just blinked uncomprehendingly and his head dropped back down onto the seat.

"Unbuckle your seat belt," she repeated, enunciating each word slowly, trying to compel his co-operation.

The man reached a bit farther towards her with one hand, clawing at the seat in another futile attempt to drag himself out of the car.

"The seat belt!" she urged again, but he just collapsed prone on the seat with a soft groan.

Great. Just great. She'd have to undo it herself. Swallowing nervously, she crawled carefully into the car. Placing hands and knees gingerly on pearls of broken glass, she inched forward, praying fervently that the car wouldn't choose that moment to slip over the cliff. Clutching the steering wheel with her right hand, she edged forward, shoved her left arm under his torso and groped blindly for the latch she knew was under there somewhere. Pebbles of broken glass gouged into her belly as she strained to reach the buckle.

The car shifted.

Amy's scream faded into a little whimper as she lay frozen in place, shaking, her heart thundering in her ears. She stayed that way for long moments, afraid to move, listening to the little rocks tumbling down, down, until they couldn't be heard anymore. Time stood still as the silence pressed down on her.

Amy gritted her teeth and forced herself to move. She had to get out quickly but she couldn't abandon this man either. Using all her strength she shoved her arm a little farther under his body. Sweat beaded her forehead as she struggled to reach the seat belt latch. The smell of fear, blood, and pinesap permeated the air. She strained forward. So close...she could almost...reach.

As if finally understanding what she was trying to do, the man lifted himself up a bit and her hand lurched forward to contact the buckle. She pressed the release button and saw the belt slide away. Wriggling backward as fast as could, Amy extricated herself from the car. Kneeling in the gravel beside the car, she fought down a wave of nausea, and exhaled a silent word of thanks. She gulped a few breaths of air to steady herself before turning her attention back towards the driver.

"Okay. Take my hand," she instructed firmly, reaching towards him.

He raised his head. Still appearing dazed, he regarded her a moment, his breathing shallow and rapid. Slowly, his eyes began to drift closed.

"Take my hand," she demanded again, trying to keep the tremor out of her voice.

He blinked slowly, as if trying to focus, then shifted his weight fractionally and grabbed her wrist with one hand. Amy grasped his wrist with both of her hands and braced her feet on the door frame.

The car shifted again.

She gasped and held her breath for a long agonizing moment as more dirt tumbled down the escarpment. Forcing herself to breathe, she repositioned her feet on the door frame and pulled, praying constantly that the car would stay put until they were free of it.

He grabbed her arm firmly. He groaned and his shoulders bunched as he used her for leverage to pull himself towards the door. It was hard to see in the deepening gloom but she sensed his far leg was injured, perhaps trapped, because for a moment he didn't move. An agonizing groan tore from him as he gave one final heave and wrenched himself out of the driver's seat.

She shifted her position, catching him under the arms as he collapsed against her. Heaving with all her strength she dragged him free of the car and eased his head and shoulders to the ground where he lay on his back, panting, eyes closed, pain etched into his face. She felt a shiver run through him.

"It's okay. You're going to be okay," she said, trying to convey a sense of calm she was barely clinging to herself. "Think, girl, think," she whispered. "What would you do if he were an injured animal someone had just brought in?"

Forcing herself to think, Amy began a quick but thorough head-to-toe exam. Starting at the top of his head, she gently but firmly felt for bleeding and broken bones, taking mental notes as she went: laceration and lump left forehead, bleeding, but not severe. Left thigh soaking wet, probably blood, no obvious breaks. She'd need a better look at that leg.

"I'm just going to get my first aid kit from the truck. I'll be right back," she told him. His eyes opened briefly then closed again. His shivering was more pronounced now and Amy knew shock was setting in. She had to stop the bleeding from his leg and get him to a hospital quickly.

She ran to the truck, grabbed her first aid kit and flashlight, and returned to his side. Kneeling down, she opened the kit and grabbed a pair of emergency scissors. Deftly, she cut open his pant leg from ankle to hip, exposing a deep ragged gash in his thigh which bled even more freely without the pressure of the jeans to hinder it. Amy grabbed a thick absorbent pad from her kit and a couple of triangular bandages to hold it in place. He sucked his breath in with a wince as she tightened the last bandage.

"Sorry, " she said softly, feeling guilty for hurting him further. "Come on. Let's get you into my truck."

The pain seemed to have partially revived him. His face was pale but his eyes were focused for the moment. She helped him to sit up then pulled his arm across her shoulders.

"Can you stand? Try now. You've got to help me," she coaxed. He was quite a bit taller than she, but her shoulder fit nicely into his armpit and she was strong for her petite five foot four.

Using his good leg to lift himself, and leaning on her heavily for balance, he managed to stand up, and together they hobbled over to her truck. The distance seemed farther than she remembered it, and Amy realized if he were any larger, she wouldn't have made it.

He swayed as she opened the truck door. She put her arm around his waist and eased him into the passenger side where he collapsed back against the seat, breathing shallowly.

"Next stop, hospital! " she said reassuringly, leaning across to buckle his seat belt.

"No!"

Amy gasped when his hand gripped her wrist with a strength she wouldn't have thought possible. Her green eyes met his deep blue ones, and she froze, immobilized by their intensity. An electric shock jolted her, to her very soul.

"No," he repeated more softly. He loosened his grip on her arm slightly, as if realizing he was frightening her. "Please..." he panted, "no hospital. This isn't... not an… accident". His eyes drifted shut again and pain marred his face. Still, he maintained his grip on her arm as he muttered, "They know... they know... trying to… kill me." His gaze locked on hers once more. She saw his fear. "Please," he whispered. "Don't let them... find me."

Chapter Two

His eyes struggled to hold hers. In the light of the truck cab, she could see the sheen of a cold sweat on his brow. His hand shook and his breathing became more ragged as he gripped her arm.

"Please..." He seemed to be losing his fight to remain conscious.

"Okay, no hospital. I promise." She couldn't believe she was actually saying that.

A flicker of gratitude appeared briefly in his eyes just before they closed. His hand slid off her arm as his body went limp and his head slumped back against the seat. Amy walked around the truck in a daze and climbed into the driver's seat. Her hands shook as they gripped the steering wheel just a little too tightly. Thoughts warred in her head as she automatically started up the truck and pulled out onto the road.

Why had she said that? Why had she promised a severely injured man *not* to take him to the hospital when that was so obviously exactly where he should go? She must be crazy! Her thoughts tumbled around in her head as she drove down the road.

He seemed to believe someone was trying to kill him, and that if he went to the hospital they would find him there. Could there be any truth to his fear? He had smacked his head pretty hard in the accident. Maybe it was all just some kind of delusion brought on by head injury. She glanced over at his unconscious form slumped in the seat beside her. Blood already soaked through the bandage she had applied to his leg.

Amy chewed on her lip as she struggled within herself.

He needed a hospital. That leg needed stitches. He had a head injury for heaven's sake! But what if he was right? Unconscious in a hospital bed, he'd be an easy target if someone wanted to finish off what they'd started.

The local hospital was small. They didn't have enough staff to have him watched constantly, assuming they even believed such a wild story. The sheriff, Dale Johnston, was an old family friend, but he still considered her a kid and couldn't see her as the thirty-year-old medical professional she was. She was sure he wouldn't believe her. Even if he did, there were only two, inexperienced deputies who had to work the dayshift and couldn't stay up all night doing guard duty as well.

They probably wouldn't take her story seriously. Even she was having a hard time believing it and she had seen the fear in his eyes.

And what if this guy was dangerous? She looked at him again and a surge of protectiveness welled up within her. He didn't look like much of a threat at the moment, unconscious in the seat beside her. He'd begged her for help. How could she turn her back on someone who needed her so desperately? She remembered only too well the pain of being abandoned in her moment of greatest need. She couldn't do it, not even to a stranger.

"God," she prayed aloud. "What should I do? He needs a hospital!"

You have a hospital. The thought floated through her mind and wouldn't leave her be.

"But I'm just a vet. That's not the same as a hospital."

The urge to take him to her practice didn't lessen.

She knew what she was capable of. She had the knowledge and the skill to stitch up that leg, plus she had the clinic and all the supplies necessary. Only last week she had stitched up the Colliers' horse when it had ripped open its leg on a barbed wire fence. This wasn't much different than that.

What she didn't have was any way of knowing if this was the right thing to do.

Do you trust Me?

She thought for a moment. Did she trust God? Really trust Him?

"Yes Lord. I do."

She turned left at the main road, heading towards home and away from the town and hospital.

* * *

Amy pulled her truck into the parking area in front of her clinic, stopping as close to the door as she could. As she got out of the truck she could see Bella, her Golden Retriever, bouncing up and down in her kennel like a jack-in-the-box, barking joyously.

"You're going to have to wait awhile, Darlin'," Amy told her in a grim voice. "I've got my work cut out for me."

Amy's veterinary clinic was located within her old house just outside of town. The house's main front door opened straight into the clinic waiting area. Amy marched inside, flicking on banks of lights as she went, and proceeded through the waiting area into the surgical room beyond. Grabbing her lab coat off the hook, she whipped her hair back into a ponytail with the elastic she kept in the coat pocket. Pushing aside all the doubts and what-ifs that still clamored for attention in the back of her mind, she morphed into professional mode and rapidly readied the surgery room for what was to come.

She cranked the heat up; he was already chilled, no need to make it worse. Then she gathered her supplies and adjusted her surgical table to the right height. She looked at it critically, judging its size. Yes, it would be large enough, just barely. Her usual patients were quite a bit smaller than a fully grown man. Everything was ready to go within a few minutes.

Amy returned to the truck.

This wasn't going to be easy she realized as she opened the truck door. He lay as she had left him, slumped back with his head against the seat, his face turned towards her and his eyes closed. She watched the pulse beat rapidly at the base of his throat. Too rapidly. No time to waste.

"Come on, Darlin', wake up," she said urgently, shaking him gently. "You need to walk one more time. Just one more time." She shook him again, a bit more firmly, while part of her brain noted with amusement that she was calling him Darlin' now just like she did her dog.

Shut up! she told herself silently as her brain began to giggle hysterically in the background.

"Wake up!" She shook him even more firmly and was finally rewarded as he groaned softly and opened his eyes a crack. "We've got to get you into the clinic. Come on, were almost there."

He mumbled something incomprehensible, but he lifted his head and leaned forward so she could pull his arm around her shoulders and slide her arm around his waist. She grasped his belt tightly so as to have a solid grip on him, then helped him slide off the seat. He gasped when his leg touched the ground but she steadied him and somehow they stumbled into her clinic. She eased him down onto the surgical table, helping him lift the injured leg up and making sure he was centered.

* * *

He swam through a sea of pain. Fire lanced through his leg with every movement, like red hot razors, slicing from his knee into his groin. His head throbbed with each beat of his heart, like someone was pounding on it with a mallet. Infusing everything was an overwhelming sense of fear, almost panic, though he didn't know why. There was a woman moving around, doing...something. He turned his head to see but the room tilted and began to spin crazily. A wave of nausea washed over him. He closed his eyes tightly again, but it didn't help. The room kept spinning. His stomach rolled.

What was happening? Was she cutting his pants off? He forced his eyes to open. Lights. Lights everywhere, blinding him. Where was he?

He tried to focus, his mind assaulted by the jumble of images and sensations pouring in. He felt a pinch in his arm. He cracked his eyes open, peering down his arm. The woman was taping a little tube to his arm, a tube which ran up to a small clear bag hanging from a pole. She wore a white lab coat. There was a big light right over him, shining into his eyes. He struggled to sort the images. Was he in a hospital? Panic surged to the front of his mind.

"No! No hospitals!" He tried to sit up but pain jolted through him like an electrical shock.

Gentle hands firmly eased him back down. His head turned side to side as he tried to find a way out. His breath came in ragged gasps. There were blinding lights everywhere.

"Can't stay here... can't..." He could feel his heart hammering in his head. There was a loud buzzing in his ears, like a thousand angry bees.

Someone was talking. Her. Gentle hands clasped each side of his face. What was she saying?

"Look at me. Look at me."

The words were soft, firm. He tried to focus. Green eyes. Beautiful green eyes.

"You're safe. I'll keep you safe. I promise."

Safe?… His breathing slowed. Somehow he trusted the green eyes. He had no choice. Darkness crept in around the edges of his vision and the buzzing increased, drowning out everything else. He relaxed back and let the darkness enfold him.

Safe.

Chapter Three

Amy tried to steady her shaking hands. For a moment there she had thought he was going to get right up off the table. She took the oxygen mask she had readied earlier and slipped it over his mouth and nose, turning on the flow. The gas was a mixture of oxygen and anesthetic to keep him sedated while she stitched up his leg. Gas was her best choice to keep him under, but not so far under that she couldn't get him back again.

She checked to make sure his IV line was flowing freely. Thank goodness that when God created people and animals he used the same basic building blocks to put everything together. The same fluids she used for her animal patients were also suitable for humans. She knew he had lost a lot of blood and, while she couldn't provide more blood, she could build up his blood volume by pumping him full of saline. The extra oxygen would help, too. Hopefully, she could stop the shock that had been progressing steadily since the accident. Shock could kill, and if he died she'd have a whole lot of explaining to do.

"God, *please* don't let him die," Amy prayed fervently.

She covered him with a warm blanket leaving only his left leg exposed and opened a surgery pack. Blood had completely soaked through the bandage. She removed it carefully and took a closer look at the damage. The wound was deep, more a tear than a cut, with rough jagged edges and bits of dirt in it, or, was that bark? She couldn't be sure. She clamped off a small artery to stem the flow of blood and thoroughly washed the wound. Then she began to stitch, first the artery, then the deeper levels using self-dissolving sutures. She finished the surface using a stitch stapler. It was like a staple gun, except it pinched metal stitches through the skin. It was fast, efficient, and very secure.

The worst done, Amy turned her attention to the laceration on his forehead. His dark wavy hair was caked in blood but the cut itself wasn't that bad. Amy sighed. Scalp wounds always bled profusely, but a few stitches had it pulled together nicely. Hopefully there wouldn't be much of a scar.

Amy rechecked his vital signs. Although thin and thready, his pulse was steady at least. His breathing, still a little rapid, had improved. His blood pressure was low but acceptable. All things considered, he might live.

Amy looked around the room and ran a shaky hand through her hair. Now what? She couldn't leave him lying on her surgery table, but where to put him? Her bedrooms were upstairs and trying to haul him up a flight of stairs was completely out of the question. She really didn't want him to try to walk at all, at least not until he'd had some time to heal. He didn't need that artery pulling open again. So what to do?

Amy pulled up a chair and sat down to think. She gazed at the door which linked her surgical room to the rest of the house.

The house had been an answer to her prayers. Amy thought back to the day she'd bought it. Coming back to her old home town after being away at school for so long had been difficult, especially with what had happened prior to her leaving, but she couldn't think of anywhere else she'd rather call home. She'd just graduated as a veterinarian and needed to find somewhere to live as well as a place to start her own clinic. Available office space had been almost non-existent in town, and housing there was expensive.

It had been her realtor's suggestion to combine her house and clinic in the same building. He knew of this big old house just outside of town which had been on the market for a long time. It needed some fixing up, but with a little TLC it could be perfect, and the price was right for a new graduate looking for a mortgage. Amy had loved it at first sight.

She'd turned the south half of the large main floor into her veterinary clinic. The main front door on the south side led into a waiting area with a check-in desk and the filing system behind it. There was a small exam room to the right, and the larger surgical room was towards the centre of the house. Along the east wall of the surgical room, tucked under the stairs to the second floor, were kennels of various sizes to house sick animals until they were ready to go home. The door along the north wall of the surgical room led directly into her living room.

Her kitchen and living room stretched across the north half of the house. The kitchen door opened out to the front gravel parking lot on the west side. Walking through the kitchen took you past a small bathroom, laundry room combination to the right, and into the living room. Sliding glass doors at the back of the living room opened onto a large sundeck stretching across the entire east side of the house. The deck overlooked her fenced-in yard, which sloped down from the house, and a lovely little lake in the distance. It was perfect, except she had no one to share it with.

Amy returned her gaze to the man lying on her surgical table. She had already turned off the anesthetic, leaving only the oxygen running, but he showed no sign of waking.

He really was quite handsome now that she had a moment to notice. Dark lashes fanned out over pale cheeks as he slept. He had a strong face and well-chiseled cheekbones, with a straight nose and well-formed lips. Very kissable lips, she noted with a hint of longing. His was definitely the face of a man's man yet, at the moment, he seemed so vulnerable, almost boyish. Amy tore her thoughts back to the problem at hand.

Should she call up Candace to help her move him? Candace was a smart, competent assistant, and a great friend, too, but this pushed the bounds of friendship just a little. Amy feared she wasn't making the best choices at the moment. How could she explain this to Candace, convince her to help, *and* keep her mouth shut about it? What if she told someone? What if they thought the whole thing sounded dangerous, or illegal, and called the police? Amy had dug herself in too deep now to bail out, and she couldn't risk anyone else finding out until she could talk to her patient. She had to handle this alone for now.

So, how to move him and where to put him were the big questions of the moment. 'Where' was the easiest to answer. She had one of those inflatable beds for camping. She could set that up in her living room and, since her living room was on the same floor as her clinic, there would be no stairs to worry about.

'How' was a bit trickier to solve. Amy wracked her brain for a few moments. She absolutely did not want to wake him and make him try to walk. That could tear open some of the stitches and restart the bleeding which finally seemed to have stopped.

Amy looked her patient over critically, trying to estimate his weight. She'd never been very good at that. She guessed he was about a hundred and ninety pounds. She had moved Mrs. Freeman's English Mastiff by dragging him on a blanket, and he weighed at least two hundred pounds.

"That could work," she said, getting up from her chair.

Firstly, she dug out the inflatable bed from the back of her closet and positioned it in the living room but didn't inflate it. Instead, she draped it with a blanket and a sheet and left her bike pump beside it ready to go. Then she got another old sheet and went back into the surgery room.

As gently as she could, Amy rolled the man up on one side and stuffed the blanket under him. Then she went to his other side and pulled the blanket through so it was completely underneath him. He remained unconscious. Amy turned off his oxygen and removed the mask. She could put it back on later if necessary. She clamped off his IV line and unhooked the bag, placing it by his side on the blanket. Amy lowered her surgery table as low as she could. It stopped only six inches off the ground.

With one hand protecting his head, Amy gripped the blanket firmly and began to pull. The blanket slid easily on the smooth metal surface of the table and her patient dropped the short distance to the floor with a soft thump. He grunted softly as he landed but didn't wake. Amy readjusted her grip on the blanket and, pulling from the head end, dragged her patient across the floor and into her home. After much pulling and rolling of blankets she finally had him positioned on the air bed. Amy hung the IV bag and opened the line again, then took hold of the bike pump and began pumping the air in.

Pumping steadily, Amy considered her one remaining problem. She'd been trying to come up with any other solution but the one she had. Her patient was being pumped with fluids and eventually he'd need to use the washroom. She knew he wouldn't be able to just get up and walk to it across the room. She wasn't even sure he'd wake up long enough to try. There was no help for it. He needed a catheter.

With the air mattress finally full, Amy rubbed her face with her palms. She'd done this on animals of course, but never on a person. It felt like such an invasion of his privacy. She would be horrified if their positions were reversed, but what choice did she have? Already she'd had to cut off his jeans and T-shirt in order to treat him, but so far had preserved his dignity by leaving his underwear on. All that was about to change.

Amy sighed a deep long sigh of weariness and resignation as she pulled out the scissors once more. There was no other alternative, and she completed the job in a professional and detached manner. When all was done she arranged the blankets around him and sat on the floor by his side.

"Who are you?" she whispered to his sleeping form. "Why is someone trying to kill you?"

Not for the first time, the disturbing thought occurred to her that, if someone was trying to kill him, maybe he wasn't a nice person. She sat watching him and chewing on her lip for a while. He certainly looked nice, but that didn't prove anything. Surely God wouldn't have encouraged her to help him if he was a bad person, would He? Amy wasn't sure. God did so many things that seemed incomprehensible.

"Please, Lord, give me some sort of sign that this guy is okay and not evil. If I've messed this up please forgive me and help me get out of this. I don't know if I've done the right thing or not."

She sat by his side for a long time, watching the gentle rise and fall of his chest, and second-guessing every decision she'd made that evening.

Bella's persistent barking finally penetrated Amy's thoughts. She looked at the clock and realized it was after ten and poor Bella still hadn't been fed. Amy forced herself to her feet and let Bella into the room from the back deck. Holding her collar firmly, Amy dragged her past the injured man and into the clinic to feed her

Amy looked around the room at the chaos left over from her emergency surgery. Although it was tempting, she couldn't just leave it until morning to deal with. What if Candace came in early and saw it? Reluctantly, she began cleaning up.

When she got to the blood-soaked clothes on the floor, Amy almost just stuffed them in a bag to throw in the trash but remembered something at the last moment. Carefully, she searched through all the pockets for some clue as to who the fellow was. She was disappointed to find he had no wallet. His pockets contained several fifty dollar bills and a handful of change, nothing else.

Frustrated, Amy sat back on her heels for a moment. Maybe he'd left his wallet in the car. Well, she wasn't going back there to look now. The only things preventing that car from plunging down a two hundred-foot embankment were a couple of trees that hadn't looked secure in their footing. She didn't want to go crawling into that car again even if she could see the wallet, let alone go digging around trying to find it. She stuffed the clothes into the bag and carried them out to her personal trash bin.

Amy finished cleaning and disinfecting the work area. Exhausted, she returned to the living room but paused at the door, her hand on Bella's collar to prevent the dog from rushing over to sniff her new guest.

All was as she had left it except that now there was a small orange ball of fur curled up beside the man, purring loudly. Franz, her orange tabby cat, had wedged himself between the man's arm and side. The cat briefly looked up with a serene feline smile as Amy entered, then put his head down again, purring all the while.

Amy smiled and went over to the couch. At least he had a vote of confidence from Franzie.

"Thanks, Lord, " she whispered, choosing to take it as a positive sign.

She ordered Bella to lie down at her feet. Amy pulled the throw blanket from the back of the couch around her shoulders and rested her head back against the cushion. She was determined to stay awake and watch him to make sure he would be all right.

He had a lot of explaining to do when he woke up.

Chapter Four

Amy awoke to shafts of brilliant sunlight lancing through the room. A small flock of hungry chickadees and sparrows squabbled noisily over the seeds in the feeder outside the glass door. In the distance a woodpecker hammered away at an old tree and a jay called out raucously. Amy stretched and watched the tiny dust motes floating in the air highlighted by the sun. A lazy, peaceful feeling enfolded her and she wondered for a moment why she'd fallen asleep on the couch.

She rolled languidly onto her side and let her gaze drift across the room. Chickadees on the porch rail, Bella snoozing in the sun, some guy on an air mattress, her computer desk. Amy's eyes darted back and she stared, momentarily perplexed, at the air mattress and the dark-haired man sprawled on top of it. Her mind felt like a computer with the little multicolored wheel spinning around; processing...processing.

In a rush, the previous night's events crashed over her. Amy pushed herself up with a small shake of her head. How could she have fallen asleep? Worse, how could she have forgotten last night, however briefly? She scrambled across the room to check on him, feeling horribly guilty.

"Please, God, don't let him be dead. Please, God, don't let him be dead," she muttered under her breath as she knelt down beside his still form. She placed her hand cautiously on his forehead. Warm. His breathing was quiet and regular, his color, improved. Amy let out her breath in a rush and her body sagged in relief.

Not dead, just asleep.

She ventured a look at Bella. At some point in the night her traitorous dog had abandoned her side to go lie beside him instead. Bella lay there still, her head on her paws, large brown eyes following Amy's every move as if to say, 'Don't be mad. I still love you best.' She raised her head and thumped her tail softly on the ground as Amy bent to stroke her soft, golden fur.

"Et tu, Brutus?" she inquired quietly, smiling at Franz who was currently sunning himself on the window ledge. Now both creatures had given their seal of approval to this man who had been thrust into her life.

Amy changed the IV bag which was almost empty. Then she checked his leg wound which was no longer bleeding but seemed a bit red and warm to the touch. She knew that could mean infection setting in. Amy decided to add some antibiotics to the IV solution. She placed her cool hand on his forehead again. Yes, he was warm, maybe a bit too warm. He mumbled something and turned his head but didn't awake.

Amy sighed. She had hoped he would be awake by now. The leg wound she could handle. Even infection she could handle. Head injuries, however, she knew little about. She sat by his side and ran her hand gently through his hair. The pulse in his throat beat steadily as his chest rose and fell, rose and fell. He was so vulnerable. A surge of protectiveness welled up within her as she continued to stroke his hair.

She toyed with the idea of just giving in and calling the ambulance but reluctantly abandoned that plan. If he was right, and someone was trying to kill him, then they'd surely be watching the emergency departments for him to show up. She couldn't risk taking him there unless it was the only option. So far his vital signs were stable and he seemed to be improving. Maybe he just needed sleep to heal. She desperately hoped so.

Amy glanced at the wall clock. Five minutes after seven. Candace would be arriving soon to start checking on the animals. Amy struggled to her feet and went into the clinic to get some antibiotics for her unconscious patient before Candace arrived and started asking uncomfortable questions. She added the antibiotics to one of the IV ports, locked the door between the clinic and her home, and ran upstairs for a shower.

Just over an hour later, Amy had dressed, eaten and pulled her honey blonde hair back into a simple ponytail. She'd had to force herself to eat something since her stomach seemed to be in a knot. She could hear Candace moving around in the clinic and knew she needed to get in there soon herself. She checked her patient one more time. There was no sign of him waking, yet Amy feared he'd wake the minute she was gone from the room. What would he do if he woke here, in a strange place, alone, confused? She'd stressed about it all morning.

Maybe she should just tell Candace she felt sick and have her cancel the day's appointments. But then what would she do? Sit on the couch and watch him sleep all day? She'd go nuts. Maybe it would be better to have some work to keep her busy after all. Besides, surely he'd call out if he woke up. She was only in the next room. She'd hear him. What if Candace heard him too? Amy continued to waffle until the last minute, then gritted her teeth and chose to go to work. People were counting on her.

The day dragged by. Amy kept making excuses to go into her home to check on him. He continued to sleep and run a temperature. She changed his IV and catheter bags on her lunch break, giving another dose of antibiotics when she did so.

Back in the clinic she found it difficult to focus. Fortunately, it was a fairly simple day. There was one surgery scheduled in the morning, spaying Mrs. Jacobs' cat, then just routine vaccinations and check-ups. Still, her mind was always listening for a sound which never came.

Candace, a willowy beauty with an engaging grin, kept giving her strange looks, but Amy avoided any opportunity for questions. Instead, she painted a smile on her face and chatted to her clients more than usual.

Finally, the day was almost over. Amy felt like a nervous wreck. She had to suppress the urge to grab all of Candace's belongings, shove them into her arms, and rush her out the door saying, "Nice-working-with-you-today-gotta-go-now-bye!" Instead, Amy forced herself to appear calm while Candace puttered around tidying up the last few details of the day's work.

"What is wrong with you today?" Candace asked abruptly, her golden-brown eyes flashing mischievously. Taller than Amy, she wore her dark brown hair in a pixie-cut which framed her oval face perfectly. She pinned Amy with her gaze, as if she could force a confession by staring hard enough.

"What? Nothing." Amy felt her face flush.

"Don't give me that. You've been jumpy and distracted all day. You keep running back and forth into your house, which is totally not like you. Plus, I get the distinct impression you can't wait for me to leave. What's up?"

"It's..uh.. It's just that I've got this screaming headache and... I decided to take your advice."

"My advice?" Candice sounded curious, her ever-present grin bursting forth.

"Yeah. I... uh.. signed up with one of those online dating things. I keep checking my computer to see if anyone has responded yet. I didn't want to tell you this soon, but I guess I've been pretty obvious." Amy hoped her excuse sounded plausible. It was the best she had been able to come up with in case Candace confronted her. She hated lying to her friend, but the truth was just too complicated to deal with.

"Amy, that's wonderful!" Candace gushed. "It's about time you tried to meet someone besides the local hicks."

"Yeah, well, we'll see how it goes. Candace, my head is really pounding. It's turning into a full-blown migraine. Can you please cancel tomorrow's patients before you go? Then in the morning, after Mrs. Jacobs picks up her cat, you can take off early for the weekend. How does that sound?"

"Sweet! Why don't you just go lie down? I'll finish up here and then bring Bella in for you."

"No!" Amy said sharply, quickly backtracking at Candace's startled expression. "I mean that's really nice of you, but Bella's been chasing the cat lately and I'd rather leave her outside for a while until the drugs kick in. But thank you, really," she ended lamely. "I'll just go lie down now."

Amy escaped back into her home leaving Candace to finish up. She closed the door softly and locked it before leaning back against it with a huge sigh. What a long, stressful day. She wished she could just run back in and confide everything to her friend and beg for advice.

She didn't.

Her "fake" headache wasn't a fake either, though she doubted it would become a migraine. She'd never had an actual migraine before, but she did get muscle tension headaches, and this felt like a doozy. Amy went to the kitchen for some ibuprofen and a large glass of water. She then returned to the man lying peacefully on the inflatable bed by the back wall.

"I think you've got it easier than I do right now," she told him. "At least all you have to do is lie there and sleep. I get to do all the worrying."

She was worried, too, she realized, when she began her usual check of bandages, IV lines and vital signs. Very worried. He still wasn't awake and that really bothered her. It had been less than 24 hours she reminded herself, but to her anxious mind it seemed much, much longer. A whole lifetime since the end of work yesterday. Her whole world was slightly askew. If only he would wake up. Then she could find out who was after him and connect him back to his own people and safety. Then she could get back to her old life.

"Yeah, like *that's* a ball of excitement," a nasty little voice in the back of her mind sneered. "Wouldn't want to miss 'The Simpsons' reruns would we?"

Amy pushed the nasty voice away then knelt beside her handsome stranger again and stroked his hair gently. It was damp. Good. That meant his fever had broken and the antibiotics were doing their job. She continued to stroke his hair, hoping that her touch would help somehow.

"Wake up, Darlin'," she said softly. "Wake up."

She watched the soft rise and fall of his broad, well-muscled chest with its sprinkling of dark hair. The kind of chest a girl could just lay her head against and snuggle close to, she thought. She could almost feel big strong arms wrapping her in a warm embrace, her cheek cushioned in the hollow over his heart. She suppressed an urge to run her fingers through the springy dark curls and pulled his blankets up a bit higher instead.

Amy got up with a sigh, annoyed with herself. What was she doing? Here she was mooning over him like some lovesick school girl when he was seriously injured and might never wake up. How inappropriate. How unprofessional. How human.

It was no secret that she was lonely. She had several good girlfriends, of course, and she loved her work. She met a lot of great people through her work, too. But it just wasn't the same as having that special someone in your life. She used to have someone special, she reminded herself. At least, she'd thought so at the time. Then the car accident tore her life to pieces and left her trying to rebuild a radically different future than the one she'd been counting on.

Well, she certainly wasn't going to build a new future with this guy, she told herself firmly, even if he was gorgeous. She didn't know a thing about him, except that he believed someone was trying to kill him. What kind of person had people out to kill them? Was he addicted to gambling? Maybe he owed thousands of dollars to the mob. Maybe he *was* the mob! Maybe he was a drug dealer! Or worse. Amy paced the floor while her imagination ran amok.

She plopped down on the couch and sat staring at him. He didn't really look like a drug dealer. He looked a little rugged and wild with that unshaven dark shadow along his strong jawline and the bandage on his forehead, but somehow that just made him all the more attractive. Amy gave her head a shake and arose with a snort.

"This is crazy. You wouldn't know what a drug dealer looked like if one walked up and bit you!" she said to herself. "He needs a real doctor, not me, and I need him out of here."

She crossed the room to the phone, picked it up and started to dial. She punched in five numbers, then hesitated, and finally put the phone slowly down again. She'd promised him. A promise wasn't something you broke just because it was difficult or even dangerous. Was it? Amy knew only too well the pain of having someone you were counting on bail out when you needed them most. She picked the phone up again. She put it down. She paced.

Finally, in frustration, Amy scribbled a quick note telling her patient to wait here and she'd be right back. She grabbed a warm jacket and headed outside onto the sundeck where Bella greeted her joyously. She hoped that, after lying unconscious for nearly 24 hours, he'd wait a bit longer before waking.

"Come on, old girl. I need a game of fetch and so do you."

Amy jogged down the stairs into the back yard. She found Bella's tennis ball and hurled it towards the back of the yard. The dog bounded off joyously, barking her excitement and diving into the brush. Amy turned her face towards the east, allowing the wind to blow her hair back. The September sun hung low in the sky and the leaves were just starting to turn, although a few early ones had fallen already.

Amy lobbed the ball again and again, hands stuffed into her pockets to keep them warm between throws. A cool breeze caressed her face as if trying to wipe away the anxiety that clung to her. She tried to clear her mind, to calm down so she could think straight. She also prayed as she breathed in the sweet, pine-infused mountain air, talking to God about everything and begging for guidance.

Amy climbed the stairs twenty-five minutes later, chilled but calmer. She still wasn't sure what to do, but had decided to wait one more night. Bella, on the other hand, didn't seem to share her concerns. The dog, after gobbling her dinner down, stretched out on the floor beside the makeshift bed, and fell soundly asleep. Franz, too, had crept back onto the bed and curled up between the man's legs, purring softly.

Amy wished she could be just as relaxed about things, but she'd learned the hard way not to trust people too readily, especially men, and this man was even more suspicious than most. Still, there was something about him that called out to her for mercy and compassion. She wanted to trust him and to help him even though her good sense said she shouldn't.

Amy struggled to understand her own motivation while she fixed a quick supper. After eating only a small portion, she wrapped a blanket around herself and curled up on the couch where she could watch the slow rise and fall of his chest.

* * *

Amy struggled to wake up as if swimming to the surface from somewhere deep under water. She felt sluggish and groggy, but pushed herself into a sitting position. Something had woken her. Sunshine streamed in through the windows and hurt her eyes as she looked owlishly around the room. Her house guest was still lying on the bed in the corner. Had he changed positions in the night? She couldn't be sure but she didn't think he was the reason she'd woken up.

A muffled thump and voices in the other room made her jump slightly. She realized it was Candace taking care of things in the clinic. She guessed Mrs. Jacobs had arrived to collect her cat. That must have been what woke her.

Amy got up and went to check on the man. Kneeling beside him, she placed her hand on his forehead which felt warm but thankfully not hot. She ran her fingers through his hair a couple of times, willing him to wake up. He remained quiet and still, his breathing soft and regular.

She was getting very tired of thinking of him as "that man" or her "patient". It would be very nice, she thought, to have a name to think of him by. She wondered what it might be as she changed the IV bag. She'd have to get more antibiotics later, once Candace had gone, since she'd forgotten to get some last night.

Amy stood over him, watching him. She sighed. If he didn't wake up soon she'd have to call the ambulance, promise or no promise. How on earth was she going to explain this to the sheriff?

"Please, God, please make him wake up," she prayed silently.

Her eyes drifted out the glass door which overlooked the lake. It was going to be a nice day today. A scattering of high thin clouds sat in an icy blue sky, the trees swayed gently in the breeze, and her regular flock of songbirds squabbled over the bird feeder on the deck. It was the perfect day for a long walk with Bella. Too bad she'd be stuck inside pretending to have a migraine.

Her eyes darted back to the man at her feet. Had his hand just moved? No. Just her imagination.

Amy headed to the kitchen. She ate a little cheese melted on bread while she sipped her coffee and was soon feeling a little more awake. She stretched as she got up from the chair, her back stiff from sleeping on the couch two nights in a row, and returned to the living room.

Bella was fussing at the door so Amy let her out onto the deck. Franz zipped out, too, as the door was opened.

"You leave those birds alone, you old hair-ball," she called after him.

He looked back briefly with a twitch of his tail then disappeared down the stairs and into the brush.

Amy walked over to where the man lay and knelt down beside him. She pulled the blanket off his leg and carefully removed the bandage, pleased to see that the redness along the stitches was fading. She placed her hand gently beside the wound. His leg felt warm but not the heat of infection. She added some ointment and gently re-bandaged his leg, smiling to herself.

She moved the blanket back over his legs again, then checked his head wound. The cut wasn't bad but there was a huge purple goose-egg behind it. No wonder he was still off in la-la land, she mused. There was serious bruising all down his left arm and chest too, probably from when he and the car slammed into those trees.

Amy gently ran her hand along the bruises on his arm. She touched his side, feeling along his ribs with her fingertips to see if there were any signs of broken bones she might have missed earlier. So much bruising.

Her hand trailed across his abdomen until it came to rest on the line of hair descending from his chest to his navel. Giving into temptation, she ran her fingers up through the soft springy hairs to his chest, reveling in the feel of them.

She let her eyes drift back up to his face, then gasped and snatched her hand back with a jerk.

A startling pair of deep blue eyes regarded her with amusement.

Chapter Five

The man lay on the makeshift bed, watching her, a smile playing at the corners of his mouth. Amy couldn't seem to pull her eyes away; his eyes held her immobile with their intensity.

"I... uh... I was just... um... checking your bandages," she stammered, feeling her face flame.

His smile broadened as he replied in a slightly raspy voice, "Well, don't let me stop you. I was kind of enjoying it." He chuckled softly, then winced.

Her face warmed even further.

Amy tore her gaze away, stood, turned and began fiddling with the IV bag to hide her embarrassment. He was laughing at her! How *dare* he?! After all she'd been through, all she'd done for him, he finally woke up, and he had the nerve to *laugh* at her!

Then it hit her.

"You're awake!" She turned back towards him as her legs folded beneath her and she collapsed into a kneeling position beside him. Relief flooded through her like a tidal wave, overwhelming her. She repeated softly, "You're awake."

She sat there, grinning foolishly, totally lost for words until, inevitably, the emotional dam cracked and she burst into tears. Amy dropped her face into her hands, all the fear and anxiety she had bottled up, all the self-doubts and worry she'd reined in, broke forth and it all came rushing out at once.

After a moment, Amy managed to calm herself enough to notice her patient was making consoling noises and patting her gently on the knee.

"Hey, don't cry. I was just teasing you a bit," he coaxed, looking worried.

"I'm sorry," she said, drawing a ragged breath. "It's not that... It's just... I thought... I thought you might never wake up. I thought you might die, and I'm just so relieved to hear you talking and, and..."

Just when she thought she might start crying again he squeezed her knee and said, "I'm fine, really. I'm totally fine. See?"

With that he attempted to roll over, but the moment he moved his leg, he sucked in his breath sharply and the color drained from his face. Amy instinctively leapt forward to help him ease his leg back down onto the bed. He held his breath, his eyes closed tightly and muscles tensed until he was settled again. He took a few deep breaths while the color returned to his face.

"Okay," he gasped, his voice strained. "Maybe not *totally* fine... but I'm not gonna die... I don't think."

After a few moments he opened his eyes again and added, "Man, that hurt! What happened to me?"

"You were in a car accident. Your car went off the road and hit some trees. You have a really deep gash in your thigh which you've just noticed, plus you hit your head pretty hard. I stitched your leg up, and your head, too, and started the IV line. You've been unconscious for over thirty-six hours, which was starting to freak me out. That's why I've been so scared. That's why I kind of lost it just now."

Amy realized she was babbling and shut up, still feeling flushed. While she was talking he'd been looking around the room, at her , the IV pole, at everything he could see without moving too much.

"Is this your house?" he asked.

"Yes."

"And you did all this by yourself?"

"Uh-huh."

"How? Where did you get this stuff? "

"I'm a vet."

"A vet?"

"Yes. A veterinarian. My clinic is in the next room. Everything I needed was right there. Everything including pain meds!" she said with dawning horror. "I am so stupid.

Your leg must be killing you and I've given you nothing. I'm so sorry. Would you like something for pain?"

"Actually, yeah, that would be good."

Feeling horribly guilty, Amy unlocked the door and poked her head into the clinic. There was no sign of Candace. She was probably up front, finishing the paperwork, Amy surmised. She crossed the room quickly to the medicine cabinet and grabbed a package of pain pills and another dose of antibiotic. Hurrying, she ducked back into her living room before Candace could catch her. She didn't want to lie to her friend and yet, she wasn't ready for long explanations either.

Amy quickly fetched a glass of water from the kitchen and returned with a couple of pills in her hand. She helped support his head with one hand as he swallowed them, then eased him back down. This time she made sure to keep her touch completely professional. Even so, she was acutely aware of his nearness, and the way he was looking at her had all her nerves tingling. She was glad the blankets had been pulled up higher across his chest. Even all battered up, he looked way too sexy for her own good.

"I don't mean to sound ungrateful," he said, "because I am, grateful I mean, but why didn't you just call an ambulance?"

Amy gave him a long, flat, look before responding. "I wanted to, believe me, but you wouldn't let me. You begged me not to, in fact. Don't you remember?"

It was obvious from the blank look he was giving her that he didn't. She wasn't sure she wanted to burden him with all the details of someone sabotaging his car and trying to kill him. He had enough to deal with at the moment she decided. That kind of information could wait.

"Oh well," she said , trying to sound positive. "It's a long story. I'll fill you in later. The important thing right now is to get you back wherever it is you belong. I'm Amy, by the way. Amy Scott."

"Nice to meet you, Amy Scott," he said with a tired smile.

With a stab of regret she realized she'd never get to know the owner of that smile. He'd only just woken up and already she felt charmed by his smile and the sense of humor he seemed to have, even in this difficult situation. She wished she could have just a little more time to get to know him before having to say good-bye. That wasn't going to happen though. She'd be calling the sheriff in a few minutes, now that he could explain for himself what was going on, and soon he'd be gone from her life and back to his own. It would be for the best she told herself firmly.

Herself wasn't so sure she agreed.

"And you would be...?" Amy prompted, letting the question trail off.

He opened his mouth to answer, then stopped. She watched as the smile on his face slowly faded. His brow furrowed slightly and he seemed to be searching for the answer. He turned his face away from her, and just stared at the wall for a long time.

"I don't know."

His words were so faint Amy could barely make them out.

"Pardon?"

"I...don't know," he repeated, his voice flat, controlled.

"Seriously?" She couldn't keep the slight edge out of her own voice.

He glanced back at her, rubbed his face with his right hand then dropped his forearm across his eyes. He swallowed hard.

"I can't remember anything. Nothing before waking here in this room."

"You can't be serious. You have to remember *something*. How am I going to get you home if you can't remember anything?" Her voice rose slightly.

"Sorry to inconvenience you!" he snapped, dropping his arm to glare at her. He turned his face away again.

Being a vet, Amy was used to working with patients who couldn't tell her what was wrong with them. She was used to reading body language and subtle nuances of expression to gauge pain and emotion. She saw the little muscle twitching at the angle of his jaw. She noted the tension in his shoulders as his hands clenched the blankets. She saw the look in his eyes before he'd hidden it from her. Where someone else might have heard anger in his words, she had heard something else.

All at once, Amy felt ashamed of herself. If this was hard for her, having this strange man in her home, how much worse was it for him? He'd woken up, battered and bruised, in a strange place with no memory of who he was or where he belonged, and on top of it all, she was upset with him. How selfish she was. Yet she knew he wasn't angry. Though he was trying hard not to show it, he was scared.

Amy stared down at her hands for a moment, unsure, and then she reached out hesitantly and took one of his hands in hers. He turned to look at her, scowling, glanced at their hands then back at her face.

"No. I'm the one who's sorry. This isn't your fault at all and I didn't mean to snap at you. It just never occurred to me that you might not remember anything. But... you did get a pretty hard smack on the head, so it does make sense that you've lost your memory for a bit. It'll come back though. I'm sure of it. In the meantime, you can stay here as long as you need to. Rest. Heal. Take your time. We'll work it out together." She smiled warmly and gave his hand a small squeeze.

He regarded her solemnly for a moment before responding. "Thanks," he said simply. He then lifted her hand and kissed the back of it softly, his lips barely touching her skin.

Amy flushed, confused, as a little thrill ran up her arm. He was stirring up all kinds of emotions best left alone.

"It's too bad you don't remember your name. I need to call you something besides 'Hey you'," she laughed, trying to cover her discomfort.

"Got any suggestions?" he asked, a hint of amusement returning to his voice.

"How about John, as in John Doe?"

He made a face. "Too clichéd."

"We could go with something biblical. Matthew? Mark? Luke? There's John again. How about Moses?"

He chuckled quietly, and then winced, "No, not Moses. Mark doesn't sound too bad though."

"All right. Mark it is. Are you hungry, Mark?"

"Now that you mention it, yeah, I could go for a little something."

"How does scrambled eggs and toast sound?"

"Sounds great," he replied.

* * *

Mark watched as she walked out of the room into the kitchen. He sighed and rubbed his face with one hand. His whole body throbbed but it was bearable as long as he didn't try to move. A deep weariness made his body feel heavy and sluggish. He wanted to just close his eyes and sleep. Maybe when he woke up everything would be normal again, whatever normal was.

Dishes clanked in the kitchen and his stomach growled in response. He really was hungry. That must be a good sign. He hoped so, anyway.

He tried again to remember something, anything. Vague images drifted just beyond his ability to recognize them. Like when there is a word on the tip of your tongue but you can't seem to speak it, his memories teased him, yet remained unreachable. He tried to calm the frustration that welled within him, knowing it wouldn't help him remember.

Mark closed his eyes and decided to think about the only thing he could remember at the moment. Amy.

It had been fun to watch her while she didn't know he was awake. He remembered the touch of her hand on his side and how it felt as she ran her fingers through the hair on his chest. He remembered her embarrassment and how pretty she looked when she blushed. He remembered her smile and how it seemed to make her face almost glow. He remembered the green of her eyes and how they seemed to look right into his soul.

A flash of memory hit him. Green eyes, those same green eyes, and lights, very bright, and words. Someone saying "You're safe." Safe, safe, safe, echoing. A surge of nameless fear engulfed him.

Mark opened his eyes abruptly, his pulse racing. He ran both hands through his hair and stared at the ceiling for a few minutes as he tried to calm his breathing.

Well, at least he'd remembered *something.*

Amy entered the room holding a tray containing eggs, toast, and orange juice. "Are you okay?" she asked with a note of concern in her voice.

"Yeah, fine," Mark lied. He wasn't sure why, but he didn't want her to see his fear. He covered it with a rakish grin. Amy set the tray on the coffee table and turned back to him, moving with the fluid grace of a dancer.

"If I prop up a bunch of pillows here against the wall, do you think you could slide back a bit and sit up to eat?"

"Sure, no problem," he lied again, trying not to think of how much that leg had hurt the last time he moved it.

"Okay, I'll help. Sit up first, then use your good leg to push and just slide the sore one. Oh, and be careful not to pull on the catheter."

She had already helped him into a sitting position but with her last words of caution, he froze. She couldn't possibly have just said what he thought he'd heard.

"The what!" He stared, horrified, into her amused eyes.

"The, um, catheter," Amy said as a smile toyed at the corners of her mouth.

He lifted the blankets cautiously and looked underneath. Now it was his turn to feel his face flush as he sat staring, at a loss for words. The laughter dancing in her eyes didn't help either. So much for acting tough. She'd apparently seen him unconscious, bleeding and buck naked, too. It couldn't get much worse than that, except for having *tubes* stuck into places they didn't belong. Perfect. Just perfect.

Finally he blurted, "That thing has got to go," and, as an afterthought, "Where are my clothes?"

Amy seemed to suppress a giggle as she answered, "I'm sorry. You just look so...so offended." She continued still smiling, "I'm afraid I ruined your clothes. I had to cut them off to treat you. I'll go out later and get you something to wear. As for the catheter, it was necessary while you were unconscious. We can take it out later if you want, but it might be useful to leave it in until you can walk to the bathroom."

"No. It's definitely going. Now," Mark insisted firmly.

"After you eat." Amy was just as firm.

Mark scowled at her, but Amy just folded her arms and stared him down. Her cool green eyes had become as hard as steel. The set of her face, though kind, said she was absolutely not going to budge on the issue. Reluctantly, Mark gave in. He couldn't remove it without her help and he could see she wasn't going to change her mind any time soon.

Gritting his teeth and clutching the blanket to his waist, he slid himself gingerly up the bed. Pain lanced through his bad leg as he moved. He leaned back against the pillows feeling slightly nauseous. Amy placed the tray on the bed as she knelt down beside him.

"Are you okay? You look really white."

Mark forced a smile and nodded, not trusting himself to speak.

Amy frowned as if worried but went back to the kitchen to bring out her own plate. They ate together, in silence, each lost in their own thoughts.

Now that he had satisfied his hunger, the mind-numbing weariness Mark had been fighting began to win out. Amy must have seen it because she collected his tray and then helped him slowly, carefully slide back down the bed to lie down.

Despite her gentle help, his leg screamed at him, stabbing at him ruthlessly with every movement. He bit back a curse and held his breath instead until he was settled. She fussed around, wiping the sweat from his brow, fixing his pillow and tucking the blankets around him. In spite of the pain, the attention felt kind of good. As he drifted off, he thought she said something about calling the sheriff, but, at that moment, he just didn't care.

Chapter Six

"Amy Scott! Are you a dang fool?" Sheriff Dale Johnston's harsh words were softened by the look of concern on his face. He was about five foot ten with a stalky build, and still fit in spite of his age. After being the sheriff in town for over thirty years, he expected to know what was going on at all times and took a very dim view of people trying to slip something past him.

Amy had known Dale for years, since she was a little girl. He'd been a friend of her mother's in high school and the two had stayed in touch over the years. Now, approaching sixty and ready for retirement soon, he was speaking to her like she was still that same little kid he'd once known and not a grown woman with a doctorate.

His salt and pepper mustache bristled as he continued, "You have no idea who this fellow is yet you bring him here, right into your home, without even calling me first!"

"I've called you now," she replied defensively, sounding childish in spite of herself. This wasn't going the way she had planned. She had hoped to explain everything to him calmly, over a cup of coffee in the kitchen, while

Mark slept. She had even waited somewhat impatiently until Candace left for the day before calling him. She hadn't counted on him nearly blowing a gasket upon entering her kitchen and glimpsing the impromptu hospital ward in the next room.

"Oh, you've called me now, have you? Why didn't you just call an ambulance when you came across the wreck?"

"I forgot my phone at home. I..."

"Then you should have just driven him to the hospital!" Dale was pacing the kitchen, gesturing wildly with his arms. "What were you thinking bringing him here?"

"He asked me not to take him to the hospital. I..."

"And so you just brought him here? Because he *asked* you to? No better reason than that? And you've been playing doctor! Except you ain't no doctor, Amy, you're a vet. You're a real good vet, I'll give you that much, but you're still a vet. And you've been holed up in here trying to do this all alone. You've only called me now because the guy can't even remember his own name and you don't know what to do.

"You should have called me right away, Amy! Right away!

"What if he'd died here in your house? You could be up for manslaughter charges. As it is he could still sue you for malpractice! He could sue your butt off, little girl!"

Amy had been trying to interrupt, to explain somehow, but she had only managed to look like a dying fish with her mouth opening and closing and no sound coming out. Dale's threat of a lawsuit shocked her completely silent however. She'd never even considered that a possibility. She could lose everything. Amy tried to blink back the tears as Dale's rant continued until a voice from the living room interrupted.

* * *

"I'm *not* going to sue her," Mark yelled, crossly. Who was this guy berating Amy like that? He'd awakened to angry voices in the kitchen and, while he felt marginally better, he was still tired and sore and very cranky. He barely knew his pretty rescuer, but he'd already decided he liked her - a lot - and he didn't appreciate this guy yelling at her.

"Oh, you're awake are you?" Dale growled, striding into the living room.

"Kinda hard not to be," Mark retorted.

The two men glowered at each other across the room. Mark gritted his teeth, fuming at having to lie helplessly on the floor and stare up at the burly, if older, sheriff. He met Dale's glare directly, however, not flinching for a moment.

Amy had trailed behind Dale, hands clasped together in front of her like a chastised schoolgirl. The forlorn look on her face and the dampness around her eyes had Mark seething. He wanted to strangle Dale, sheriff or not, and he wanted to pull Amy into the protection of his arms. To his great irritation, he couldn't do either.

"So what's your name?" Dale snapped.

"Haven't a clue!" Mark snapped back.

"I hear you crashed your car up on Summit Road. That true?"

"That's what I've been told."

"And you can't remember nothing?"

"Not a single thing."

"If you lay one hand on young Amy here I'll..."

"She saved my life!" Mark interrupted.

The two men scowled at each other as, slowly, an understanding grew between them. Mark could appreciate the suspicion written all over Dale's face. Amnesia? Come on! Come up with a better line than that to weasel your way into her house. Mark had to admit it was pretty lame. Unfortunately, it was true and there was nothing he could do about it. Still, he knew he'd feel the same way Dale did if their roles were reversed.

Mark watched as Dale's eyes narrowed, assessing him. He saw the moment Dale decided to give him the benefit of the doubt, however grudgingly. As if on some silent cue, the glaring match ended.

Dale strode over to the chair and retrieved a small digital camera from his jacket pocket. Striding back, he positioned himself to take Mark's picture.

"Wait!" Amy blurted out of nowhere. "What are you doing?" She grabbed at Dale's arm.

"What I'm doing," he said, scowling and lifting the camera out of her reach, "is trying to take this fellow's picture so I can put an APB out on him and find out who he is. Someone's bound to recognize him." He raised the camera again.

"No! You can't!"

"Why not?" Mark and Dale asked, almost in unison.

"Because someone's trying to kill him," Amy blurted. "At least, that's what he told me before passing out. That's why I didn't take him to the hospital, Dale. I thought he'd be a sitting duck there. And," she pressed on as Dale tried to interrupt, "I didn't call you because I thought you wouldn't take me seriously. I thought once he woke up he could explain it all himself. But then he didn't wake up right away. And now..." she turned towards Mark, "you don't remember any of this, do you?"

Mark shook his head slowly.

Dale stood there staring at her as irritation, disbelief and concern warred across his face. Amy seemed to be holding her breath, waiting for him to come to some sort of decision about what to do. Finally he shook his head in resignation.

"All right, Amy girl. You'd better go back to the beginning and give me all the details." Dale pulled a notepad out from the front of his shirt, still looking grim, but calmer and ready to get down to business. He dragged over a chair from the kitchen, and sat down to take notes.

Amy sank down on the couch and began to talk. Mark listened intently as she relayed the previous night's events. Sitting with her arms crossed in front of her and her knees tucked up, she mostly talked to Dale, but glanced frequently in Mark's direction as if to gauge his reaction.

Mark gazed at her intently but she wouldn't make eye contact with him. He watched the emotions chase each other across her face as she relived that night. It was hard to believe she'd done everything she said all by herself. He could see she'd been scared to death, yet she'd helped him anyway. When he'd said 'she saved my life' he hadn't fully understood the truth of it.

He did now.

"What exactly did he say in the truck?" Dale asked.

Amy rolled her eyes up to the ceiling as if searching for the words there. "He said that the accident wasn't an accident and that 'they knew' and were trying to kill him. Then he said 'Please, don't let them find me'." Her eyes met Mark's, briefly.

Mark kept his expression blank. What on earth was he mixed up in? How could she be so brave as to let herself get dragged into the middle of it? Most infuriating of all, how could he not remember any of this?

"Did he say who 'they' were?" Dale interrupted his thoughts.

"No."

"Who else knows he's here?"

"No one. It was dark by the time I got him back here. I thought it was safer if I just did everything myself. Candace was a little suspicious on Thursday because I kept running back in here, but I told her I was checking my email. She thinks I've joined some on-line dating thing. I don't think she suspects the truth."

"I hate to admit this, Amy," Dale said, shaking his head, "but you may have done the best thing under the circumstances. You still should have called me right away though! But I can see what you were trying to do.

"What we do now depends on the answer I get to this next question. Can Mark, or whatever his name is, stay here with you until I figure out what's going on?"

"Yes." Amy hesitated only briefly. "As long as it takes."

Dale turned to Mark. "You okay with that?" At Mark's slight nod he continued, "All right then. Mark, you stay here. Keep your head down and don't let anyone see you. If you need anything, Amy will arrange to get it for you. I'm still going to take your picture, but I'll check things out myself and keep it quiet. Amy, how's he doing health-wise? Does he need a real doctor or are things under control? I don't want to drag Doc Martin into this unless we have to. He'll want to run a whole pack of tests down at the hospital and then the whole town will know what's going on."

"Aside from the memory loss, he seems to be healing up okay. At least he's awake now. How do you feel?" she asked, turning towards Mark.

"I feel like I've been hit by a truck, but hey, aside from that I feel great," he snapped with a short, sarcastic laugh.

"Seriously," she said, sounding cross.

"Seriously? My head's pounding, I ache all over, I won't even get started on the leg, and apparently someone wants me dead. How am I supposed to feel?"

What he felt was completely helpless and out of control. He hated it. He wanted to get out there and find out what was going on for himself, not hide while some feeble old sheriff snooped around for him. But he couldn't. He could barely move and had no strength at all. Now, on top of that, he felt like a colossal jerk because, by the look on Amy's face, he'd just hurt her feelings with his snarly rejoinder.

"I'm sorry," Mark said, softer. "It's just... It's a lot to deal with, all at once. I don't think I need a hospital though."

She gave him a brief nod to acknowledge his apology then, stone-faced, turned to Dale and said, "I'll walk you to the door."

"Fine. I'll need you to tell me exactly where the car is. We'll just call it an abandoned vehicle and run some checks on it, too. See what turns up."

Mark heard their voices fade as they wandered out of the room. He just stared up at the ceiling. Someone wanted him dead. Who? Why? He took a deep, shuddering breath and let it out slowly. How in God's name was he going to get out of this mess?

Chapter Seven

At the kitchen door, Dale checked over his shoulder then continued in a much quieter voice. "I'll run his picture through the lists of known felons as well as missing persons. There's something screwy going on here. I don't know what, but I'll find out. I'm not sure I believe this 'I can't remember' stuff he's spouting."

"I do," Amy replied softly." You should have seen his face when I asked his name and he couldn't tell me. It shook him up. You don't think he could be a felon, do you?"

"Time will tell, won't it? You call me, Amy girl, if anything odd happens. If you want that guy outta here just say the word and I'll find a different place to stash him. Ya hear?"

"Yes, I hear. Thanks, Dale." She offered up a little half smile.

Amy described exactly how to find the car, then watched from the window as Dale walked back to his truck. 'Now what?' she wondered.

She moved to the doorway and looked back into the living room. Mark was still lying on his back but had his arm thrown up over his eyes again. 'It's like he wants to hide but has no place to hide in,' she thought to herself, her heart welling with empathy.

She knew she should be mad at him for snapping at her when she'd done nothing but help him, but she chose to let it go instead. This whole situation must be completely overwhelming for him, she thought. He was actually handling it pretty well, all things considered. Now she just had to figure out how to handle living with a very attractive man in her home without getting any silly ideas about him.

Amy'd only had one serious relationship previously and it had ended badly. Since then she'd always been too busy going to school and studying to have much time for dating. Being a Christian in a secular university, it had been hard to find men there who shared her values. Since moving back to her old home town, she had found that her years in university had changed her. The boys who had excited her in high school, left her feeling flat now. Her world view had expanded and stretched. She'd grown and matured, while they seemed to be the same teenage boys only twelve years older. She wanted more in her life than just an overgrown teenager.

Amy peered at Mark covertly. There was something about *him,* however, that she found compelling. She would have to guard her heart carefully, she realized. Eventually this guy was going to remember who he was and then he'd be gone from her life forever. There was a good chance he'd turn out to be bad news, too. Didn't nice women have a bad habit of falling for dangerous men who hurt them in the end? Amy didn't want to do that again. If only he were old or ugly this would be so much easier. With a sigh, Amy decided she'd just have to keep an emotional distance.

It was time to change the IV again so Amy popped into her clinic and rummaged around for more solution and antibiotics. It felt weird going back into her living room knowing Mark would be staying for a while. He dropped his arm to look at her as she approached.

"So, is Dale going to compare my picture with all the mug shots back at the station?" Mark asked, staring up at the ceiling again.

"What...what makes you think that?" Had he heard them?

Mark laughed, humorlessly. "It's what I would do." He looked at her directly then. "Is he?"

"Yes." There was no point in lying to him.

Mark swallowed hard and looked back at the ceiling.

"He's not going to find you there, is he?" Amy asked, trying to make the question sound light-hearted.

"No! I mean… I don't think so." Sighing, he added, "I don't know." Mark put a shaky hand up over his eyes.

Amy's resolve to remain detached dissolved. She knelt beside him and placed a hand on his arm. She could feel the tremors running through him. Softly, she said, "It's going to be all right."

He slowly lowered his hand but still didn't look at her. She rubbed his shoulder gently and continued, " Dale may seem like a bit of a redneck, but he's a good sheriff. He keeps this town on a pretty tight leash and he knows his stuff. He'll find out what's going on. Just give him a little time. Let's just focus on getting you better for now, okay?"

Mark nodded ever so slightly. Amy got up and began changing the IV bag. She drew up his dose of antibiotics and injected it into the IV port. Then she emptied the catheter bag. All the while Mark lay rigid, pointedly staring out the window, fists clenched at his sides. Amy's heart ached for him but she didn't know what to do to make him feel better.

Finally, in desperation, she sat beside his head and began running her hand gently through his hair like she had done while he was still unconscious. "What can I do to help make you feel better?"

Turning his face towards her, he closed his eyes and said, "That helps." Then he sighed as she watched some of the tension ease from his body. "I'm sorry. I guess I'm not handling this very well."

"I think you're doing great, actually."

"Really?" He finally looked at her and, with a wan smile, said, "I feel like I'm drowning and you're my life jacket."

Amy's hand hesitated at that, and then continued to stroke his hair. "I promised to help you, and I will."

"Why? Why would you risk yourself to help me?" Mark was looking at her intently now, watching her face as if to read what her words might not say. "You don't even know me. I could be on your sheriff's list of criminals for all you know. You could have easily sent me to the hospital yet here I am in your home. Why?"

"Why?" she repeated softly. "Let's just say I know what you're going through. Besides, God asked me to help you."

"God *asked* you to?" He sounded skeptical. "Like this big voice from Heaven just shouts down and says 'go help that guy in the car wreck'?"

"No." Amy laughed. "Not like that. When I found the wreck, and I realized I didn't have my phone with me, I didn't know what to do. So I prayed and asked God what to do. God spoke directly into my mind. I got the strong impression that I was to help you and take you to my clinic to treat you there. I knew I should believe you and trust Him. You think I'm crazy, don't you?"

"A little," he admitted, smiling for the first time since Dale's visit. "So, what does God sound like?"

"Oh, I don't know," she said, laughing again. "Not like George Burns or Morgan Freeman if that's what you're getting at. It's not really a voice so much as the words just show up in your mind, but you know they aren't from yourself. They're from Him. It may be different for other people but that's how God talks to me. You'll understand if it ever happens to you."

"So God asked you to help and you just said yes? Weren't you scared?"

"Of course I was scared. I still am. But I learned long ago that I'm never alone. God is always with me, helping me. I can do anything when I use His strength."

* * *

Mark stared at her for a long moment. She returned his gaze with wide, open eyes and a gentle smile. There was no hint of deceit on her face. She seemed to really believe what she was saying, as crazy as it sounded to him. She didn't act crazy though. She was smart and caring and brave. She'd helped him, a total stranger, in spite of being scared. Mark couldn't wrap his mind around it.

Amy was still stroking his hair. The touch of her fingers sent little shivers of pleasure down his spine, easing the tension in his neck and back. She turned his head to have a better look at the injured side and said, "You still have blood crusted in your hair over here. Would you like me to wash it out for you?"

"Sure," he said, glad to change the subject.

Amy disappeared and soon returned with a large bowl of warm water, some shampoo and a towel. She put the bowl beside the edge of the air mattress.

"Slide over a bit, so your head hangs over the bowl. Here, I'll help."

Mark allowed her to help ease his leg over. He'd found that, if he was careful, he was able to move without too much pain though he still held his breath.

Amy supported the weight of his head with one hand, while the other hand poured water from a cup over his hair. Adding a touch of shampoo, she gently massaged his scalp. It felt exquisite.

Mark closed his eyes as the tension ebbed out of him. The pain of moving over was well worth the pleasure he was feeling now. At first, he felt just a touch guilty for letting her do this. He was pretty sure that, given a bowl of water and a cloth, he could manage to sit up and wash his own hair. But the idea of letting this pretty woman run her fingers through his hair some more was just too tempting to pass up.

He sighed deeply, enjoying every moment. Somehow the gentle pressure of her fingertips on his scalp and the warmth of the water combined to make the ache in the rest of his body lessen. The way she cradled his head so close to her stirred a deep longing within him. He suspected it had been a very long time since anyone had cared for him in quite this way. He was sorry when she put a towel under his head and eased him back onto the bed.

* * *

As she cleaned up, Amy noticed the sun was getting low in the sky. Bella was fussing at the porch door, looking for her supper and Franz was meowing impatiently with his paws up on the window. She realized it was time she made something for her and Mark to eat, too.

Amy looked at Mark. He had rolled himself very carefully up onto his side and was lying with his head on his arm watching her with eyes half-hooded. He looked exhausted but at least he seemed more relaxed than before. There was something else there in his eyes, too. She couldn't quite define it, the way he was looking at her, but it gave her butterflies.

Amy retreated to the kitchen to fix meals for everyone, animals included. After they'd eaten, she disappeared into the vet clinic for a while to check on the few animals who were recuperating in the back kennel area. When she returned 30 minutes later, she found Bella flopped on the floor beside Mark's bed. He was sound asleep with his arm stretched out and his hand resting on Bella's back. Franz was curled up at his feet, purring loudly.

Amy stood for a while in the doorway, watching the peaceful scene in front of her. The blanket had slid down off his shoulders. He had rolled slightly forward and she could see the broad expanse of his back. Even relaxed in sleep, his muscles were well-defined under smooth skin in the dim light. His hair had dried in soft waves that curled at the nape of his neck. He looked at once, both invincible and terribly vulnerable.

Amy fought back the urge to kiss him softly, where hairline met neck. Instead, she pulled his blanket back up and backed away. She hugged herself tightly, as she tried to push down the longings struggling to be recognized deep within her soul. What would it be like if he wasn't going to leave soon? She didn't dare think about it. He would leave. There was no doubt in her mind.

Amy turned and went upstairs to her bed.

Chapter Eight

Mark was driving the black Mustang, cruising effortlessly. The sun sat low on the horizon, bathing everything in a warm, orange glow and casting long shadows across the ground. The car slowed as he pulled into town. He gazed at the buildings and the streets that stretched out before him. It all seemed so familiar, and yet, eerily strange at the same time. The buildings loomed too tall and not quite straight. The people on the street all seemed to be looking at him, yet he couldn't make out their faces.

They watched him silently. They knew something. They knew!

Mark gripped the steering wheel tightly and drove on, his pulse racing. He had to get out of here. The next light was red. He stopped, frustrated. He needed to go. He was looking for something. The light was red.

Mark looked out the side window. There was a couple there, sitting at a table at a sidewalk cafe, eating ice cream. He could see them clearly. They paused in their conversation to look back at him.

The man's long legs stretched under the table. He had a powerful build, with a handsome face framed by dark hair tinged with gray. He exuded strength and charisma as he returned Mark's gaze. The woman was also long-legged, but more delicate, with a powerful grace about her. A mass of curly brown hair cascaded about an achingly beautiful face. She looked at Mark, her blue eyes warm and inviting, the barest hint of a smile gracing her full lips. They regarded him silently, knowingly. He felt naked beneath their scrutiny.

Mark wrenched his gaze away as the light turned green. He hit the accelerator and the car leapt forward. He had to get out of here, find what he was looking for.

He turned a corner and cruised farther down the street. That's when he saw them again, that same couple from the sidewalk cafe, sitting at a bus stop. Their eyes met his wide-eyed stare as he drove past in slow motion. Mark broke out in a cold sweat. How did they get here so fast? There must be a shortcut or something. He clutched the steering wheel and stomped on the accelerator. He could feel their eyes following him as he sped away.

The Mustang left town and zoomed down the highway. Mark was searching, searching for something. He rounded a bend in the road and there they were again, standing on the shoulder. The couple watched as he drove slowly past, their eyes locked once more. Mark's heart pounded. It was hard to breathe. How did they do that? How did they get past him? Mark accelerated sharply. He had to get away.

He came to a bridge. The couple was there, standing by the railing. Their eyes followed him as he flew by. He drove past a farm. They were sitting on the fence rail, watching. Mark drove faster. He felt a bead of sweat roll down his face. He drove faster and faster but they were always there, around each bend, one step ahead of him, watching. Mark's panic swelled each time. How? How were they following him?

There they were again, up ahead by the side of the road. Enough! Mark slammed on the brakes and came to a screeching halt mere feet away from them. They stood, unflinching, as a cloud of dust roiled over them. Mark thrust open the car door and launched himself out screaming, "Who are you? What do you want?"

They just stood there, silent, smiling.

"You know something. Tell me!" Mark yelled. "Tell me! Who am I?"

The woman reached her hand towards him. Mark tried to walk closer but he couldn't seem to move. He tried again. His legs felt heavy, like they were stuck.

The woman beckoned to him. She wanted to tell him. Mark couldn't move. He watched horrified as the man placed his hands gently on the woman's shoulders. In unison their beautiful faces slowly changed, becoming gaunt as the flesh melted from their bodies, the skin stretched taut across knobby limbs and their eyes protruded grotesquely. They sank into the soil beneath their feet as Mark screamed, "No! Come back!"

Then he was there, where they'd been, but it was no longer the roadside. He was standing in a cemetery. There was a grave marker there.

Who were they? He tried to read the gravestone but couldn't make out the names. If he could just get a little closer. He tried to move but couldn't. He looked down. His feet were tangled in the roots of a tree. As he watched, the roots wrapped tighter. His heart pounded in his chest. He had to get away. The roots began to pull him down, into the ground.

He tried to scream, but couldn't make a sound. He tried to wrench free but couldn't move. A searing pain slashed through his leg. He looked down again. A tree branch gouged into his flesh as blood ran down from the wound. He tried to reach down, to pull the branch out, but his arms were tangled in more branches. He arched his body, trying to break free. As he watched, the branch in his leg ripped free with a spray of blood. Pain lanced through his body. The branch reared back and paused, dripping. Mark struggled to get away. The branch hovered, threatening, and then plunged into his leg again with an explosion of agony.

Mark jolted awake with a hoarse cry, his injured leg throbbing, his body bathed in sweat. He threw the blankets back and lay on his bed for a moment, shaking, his breathing still hard and ragged. Bella whined softly and came over to lick his face.

"Hello, girl," he whispered hoarsely, reaching up to pet her with a hand that still trembled.

He rolled cautiously to his side and reached for her, pulling her down beside him. He buried his face in her soft fur. The thought of the branch protruding from his flesh still haunted him. He tried to push it away. Instead he focused on the couple in his dream. They looked so familiar, but for the life of him, he couldn't recall who they were or where he knew them from, if they were even real to begin with.

It was a long time before he was able to drift back to sleep.

Chapter Nine

Amy started down the stairs the next morning, feeling much better for having had a decent night's sleep in her own bed. Dressed casually in jeans and a T-shirt, she told herself the touch of mascara and lipstick was just because she was feeling pale from lack of sleep and had nothing whatsoever to do with Mark. The spritz of perfume was inexplicable though, so she chose not to think about that. He is a wounded traveller and you're the Good Samaritan, nothing more, she coached herself. You're helping someone in need, that's it. As soon as he's well enough, he'll go back to his own world so don't get used to him being around. Besides, you know nothing about him. He could be completely different than you think, just like David was.

David. Well, there's proof you're a horrible judge of character. You don't want to go through something like that again. So keep your head on straight and don't confuse sympathy with something more. Men are trouble and don't you forget it.

Mark was still sleeping as she entered the living room. She paused at the bottom of the stairs to watch him for a moment. He lay half on his side, half prone, with his face turned towards her. The blankets had slid down again during the night. Now the morning sun highlighted and defined every muscle across his broad shoulders, chest, and down to his waist. He looked just like a da Vinci sketch, the beauty marred only by the deep purple bruising down his left arm and side. Three days' worth of dark stubble covered his face hiding the bruising there but emphasizing the strong angle of his jaw.

He'll have a full beard if he doesn't use a razor soon.

Bella stretched and got up from beside him. She padded over to Amy with her tail wagging gently.

"Hello, old girl," Amy greeted her softly.

Bella wandered across the room to harass Franz who was lying in a patch of sun on the floor. Amy looked back to discover Mark regarding her with sleepy eyes.

"Morning," he said softly.

"Morning," she replied. "How are you feeling?" She knelt down but kept a good distance between them.

Mark arched his back slightly, flexed his shoulders and stretched his arms just a bit. Holding the blankets to his waist he slowly eased himself over onto his back again, wincing when he moved his leg. He lay for a moment with his eyes closed then looked at her again and replied with a lopsided smile, "Stiff, sore, but a little better than yesterday. How about you?"

"Me? Um... fine." Mark's question caught her off guard. David had never bothered to ask her how she was feeling. If he had as much as a sniffle, it was all about him. It was usually all about him anyway, and Amy had been young and naive enough to play into his ego trip. That Mark had even thought to ask how she was surprised her.

Flustered, she continued, "I'll just get some stuff from the clinic then I can change your IV and empty your catheter bag, okay?."

"No. Not okay," Mark responded pleasantly but firmly.

"No?" Amy stopped halfway across the room and turned back towards him, confused.

"No. You told me yesterday you'd take this thing out. I'm awake now. I'm eating and drinking, and I'll get to the bathroom if I have to drag myself there. Come on, Amy, unhook me."

"Are you sure you're well enough?"

"Yes. Completely." He flashed her a smile while placing his hands together as if praying.

"All right. Let me get my stuff."

Amy disappeared into the clinic only to return a few minutes later with a tray full of various items. Kneeling beside the bed, she set the tray down and withdrew a pair of latex gloves which she put on. She then pulled out a large syringe with a long thick needle attached. She watched, amused, as Mark's eyes widened.

"Um... What's that for?" he asked, pulling the blankets up a little higher.

"What? This?" Amy twirled the syringe in front of him with an evil smile, then, with a chuckle, added, "Relax, this just goes into the rubber tubing. There's a little water balloon inside your bladder keeping the catheter in. Once I deflate the balloon, the catheter can be pulled out easily."

"Oh," Mark responded, looking relieved. He averted his eyes out the window still clutching his blankets.

Leaving Mark covered, Amy found the rubber port on the tubing and inserted the needle. She drew back on the syringe, draining the internal balloon. In one slow, gentle motion she pulled on the catheter and it slid free. Mark exhaled loudly and she realized he'd been holding his breath. The look of relief on his face was so comical she had to laugh softly. He looked at her sideways feigning offense, and then grinned, too.

"Better?" she asked.

"Much. Thank you. Now, how about the IV?"

"Only if your temperature and blood pressure are back to normal." She stuffed a thermometer in his mouth while she cleaned up the catheter equipment. When that was done, and his temperature read normal, she wrapped a pressure cuff around his arm. While she was taking the reading, things got crazy.

Franz, tired of being used as a chew toy, leapt up from the floor where he'd been playing with Bella, and ran right by Amy. Bella, always up for a good game of 'chase the cat', barreled after him, slamming into Amy in passing. Amy, in turn, lost her balance and, in her efforts not to land on Mark's injured leg, managed to land face first on top of his chest instead. Mark let out a startled grunt as she landed full force.

"Oh! I'm sorry. I…" Amy's voice trailed off as her eyes met Mark's. They stared at each other, faces mere inches apart, blue eyes locked on green.

She felt mesmerized, unable to move, unable to think beyond the moment. The heat from his rock hard body radiated into her being, arousing feelings long buried. She could feel his heart pounding in rhythm with her own. Her lips parted, as her breath caught in her throat. His pupils dilated slightly as a slow, wide smile revealed perfect white teeth. Amy sank deeper into his eyes, transfixed. He reached up with one hand and softly brushed the side of her cheek with the back of his fingers.

At his touch, Amy jolted back to reality. What was she doing? Putting her hands on either side of his chest, she pushed herself up and back, hard. Mark winced but his grin only broadened as her face flooded with heat.

"I'm sorry. Did I hurt you? S-stupid dog!" Amy stammered, turning her back on him to adjust her shirt unnecessarily, her heart still hammering in her chest.

"Don't apologize," he said with a chuckle. "I was enjoying myself."

Certain she was still blushing furiously, Amy grabbed Bella and escorted her outside, pausing a moment to compose herself. What was wrong with her? She had no control over her emotions whatsoever, and her brain seemed to lose its ability to be logical as soon as he was near.

"Sure, he's handsome," she muttered to herself. "That doesn't mean you have to throw yourself on him and just lie there like... like…" She didn't know what it was like but she felt like a complete idiot.

Amy kept silently chiding herself as she returned to his side and removed his IV line just a little less gently than she normally would have. Mark said nothing. He just watched her, amusement dancing in his eyes.

"There. All done," she said crisply. "I'll go make some breakfast."

* * *

As she disappeared into the kitchen, Mark rolled over to watch her go. The view was spectacular. Wavy, honey gold hair fanned over graceful shoulders, and a tiny waist flared out to a lovely rounded bottom. Her jeans formed to her curves perfectly. He sighed. Even lying on his side he could still feel the soft firmness of her body where it had pressed against him. Her scent lingered in his mind, toying with his senses.

It was going to be very difficult to be a gentleman, he realized, but he was determined that's exactly what he'd be. He and Dale had reached an unspoken agreement. Dale would help Mark, and Mark would keep his hands off Amy. Or else!

A few minutes later Amy returned with a plate of toast, jam, and fresh fruit. She set it down beside him along with a glass of water and a handful of vitamins.

"Take these," she instructed briskly. "They'll help build up your blood again. I have to go out and get a few things. Will you be okay here for a bit?" She tossed him the TV remote and put the phone by his bed. "I wrote down my cell phone number if you need me. It's only ten minutes to town so I can get back here quickly if necessary. I won't be long."

"Don't worry. I'll be fine," Mark assured her. He chuckled as she left, her cheeks still stained pink.

* * *

Half an hour later Amy was beginning to calm down. She prowled the department store filling her cart with things for Mark. She'd already grabbed some T-shirts, socks, briefs, and a pair of sweat pants and was looking for some jeans. Fortunately, she'd retained enough sense to check the size of his ruined pair in her trash bin before driving off to town. She found his size and threw a pair into her cart. Henleys were on sale so she picked up one of those and then found a warm sweater to add to her pile. The evenings were starting to get chilly.

Amy looked at her growing assortment. She knew she was probably overdoing it but she wasn't quite sure what he'd need or want. She could always return what wasn't worn, she reasoned.

Now, what do guys wear to bed? She knew most of her guy friends from college wore absolutely nothing. She hoped Mark would wear something, so she searched around until she found some light cotton pajamas.

Finished with the clothes, Amy moved on to the pharmacy department. She grabbed a toothbrush and some disposable razors, and stood staring at the shaving section trying to decide what he might actually need.

A young sales clerk came by. Pointing to a boxed set, she said, "This is really nice. You get shaving cream, aftershave and antiperspirant all in the same scent. It's on sale, too." She smiled brightly.

With no better idea what to get, Amy took the boxed set and headed off to the checkout.

Christine, a friend from church, was working the cash register. She gave Amy a speculative look as she began ringing through the items.

"What's with all the man clothes? Is there something we should know about?" she said, waving the briefs discreetly under Amy's nose.

"No!" Amy scrambled for an explanation. "They're, uh, for my cousin who's staying with my mom right now. The airline lost his stuff so I offered to pick up a few things for him."

"Why doesn't he get his own clothes?"

"Um...because he's not feeling well today. You know how you always seem to catch a bug on flights. He told me his size.

"What *are* you looking at? "Amy added. All the while she had been teasing her, Christine had kept glancing over her shoulder with an odd expression on her face.

"Those two guys over by the main doors. They came in and bought some cigarettes half an hour ago, but they just keep hanging around, watching customers come and go. I saw them yesterday too, at the diner across from the hospital. You know Alice, the waitress? She said they'd been hanging around for a couple of days, but that no one seems to know them. They're starting to creep me out."

Amy glanced over her shoulder at the exit just behind her. The two men in question seemed definitely out of place in their little town. The dark-haired one wore a black leather biker jacket and had a large gold skull ring on one hand. He was thickset with muscular arms and a beer belly. He sported a mustache and goatee under small, close-set eyes.

The other man was taller but slimmer, almost gaunt looking, with stringy blonde hair that hung into his eyes. Amy noticed letters tattooed across the back of his knuckles as he took a drag from his cigarette. He exhaled slowly and looked straight towards her. A long thin scar ran from the corner of his left eye down across his cheek.

Amy quickly turned back towards Christine. There was something about their eyes, both of them, something cold and hard. Amy didn't like the looks of either of them.

"I see what you mean. Has anyone told Dale?"

"And say what? 'Hey, Dale. Can you run off these two strangers because they're creepy even though they haven't actually done anything wrong?'" Christine made a face. "You know what he'll say. Until they *do* something..."

"Yeah, I hear you."

Amy paid for her purchases and gathered up her bags. She had to walk right past the two strangers to leave the store. She looked at her feet as she walked by, trying to keep her face averted without acting too suspicious. They stopped talking as she approached, watched her intently as she went by, then resumed their conversation when she was out of earshot. Amy shivered.

On the drive home, Amy couldn't get the two of them off her mind. Could they have any connection to Mark? Her instinct told her that they'd have no trouble sabotaging someone's car if it suited them. There was something dangerous about them. Her skin had crawled just walking past them.

How could Mark have any involvement with men like them? He seemed completely different. She wasn't afraid of Mark at all, though maybe she should be. She sensed a goodness about him in spite of the strange circumstances. Those other two were definitely not good. Perhaps she was just being paranoid and there was no connection at all. Still, she resolved to mention it to Dale the next time she saw him.

Amy entered the house through the kitchen door and dropped her purse on the table. Still carrying the shopping bags, she moved into the living room. The TV was tuned to an all news channel but sat talking to itself. Mark's bed was empty.

Chapter Ten

Amy looked frantically around the room. "Mark? Mark!" Her voice rose shrilly.

"Right here," he said, calmly. "Don't panic."

She spun around to finally see him leaning in the doorway of the bathroom, hair damp, towel wrapped around his waist. Little droplets of water still glistened on the hairs of his chest.

"I thought it would be a good idea to have a shower, but now..." He swayed slightly, looking pale.

Amy dropped her bags and almost ran to his side. Slipping under his shoulder and grabbing him around the waist, she pointed him towards the couch which was closer than his makeshift bed. Her shoulder fit perfectly under his arm and she was intensely aware of the damp warmth of his skin as it pressed against her. Delightful tingles coursed through her body where they touched. Amy swallowed nervously, doing her best to ignore those tiny thrills of pleasure, as she and Mark started slowly across the room.

The fresh scent of soap and herbal shampoo clung to him. Somehow it smelled so much more intoxicating coming off his body than it ever did in her own shower. She tried to focus on the couch, but her eyes kept drifting down towards the towel wrapped loosely about his waist. She hoped it wouldn't slip off, but she couldn't seem to stop her eyes from darting down, just in case it did.

They reached the couch and, as he sat, Amy sat with him easing him down gently. He leaned his head back, eyes closed for a moment, his face pale.

"You're not well enough to be walking around the house alone. You could have popped open your stitches or passed out and hit your head again," she scolded, trying to cover the crazy dancing of her pulse. "You shouldn't have had a shower without me!"

Mark opened one eye to look at her, the devil dancing in its depths. "What? You wanted to have a shower *with* me?"

He started to chuckle softly as her mouth dropped open. She could feel the color staining her cheeks.

"That is *not* what I meant! I meant you should have waited until I could help. No! I mean...."

Mark was laughing harder.

"Oh, never mind." Amy stood up to hide the smile that was threatening to break out on her own face. She gathered up her abandoned shopping bags and dumped them at his feet.

"What's this?" he asked, his laughter slowly fading. He sat forward to see better.

"Clothes and stuff."

"For me?" he said with a bemused expression as he began to pull things out of the bag. "You didn't have to do this."

"Well, I kind of cut up the only clothes you had aside from your shoes, so, yeah, I did have to get you something to wear. You can't go around wearing nothing but a towel." She deliberately kept her gaze averted from said towel.

"But this is so much. I...I have no way of paying you back right now, but..."

"Don't worry about it," she interrupted. "It's a gift." She felt absurdly happy about the pleased, if slightly embarrassed expression on his face. It was like a mini-Christmas and she got to play Santa. Mark pulled a T-shirt on over his head; it fit perfectly. "I'll just go make some lunch so you can put the pants on."

When she returned fifteen minutes later, Mark was sitting on the couch wearing the sweat pants with his bad leg propped up. She handed him a sandwich and orange juice.

"What are you watching?" she asked, taking a seat in the armchair.

"More news. I've been watching news since you left this morning."

"Anything interesting going on?"

"Nothing that helps me. I've watched four different channels. There's no mention of any missing persons at all."

"You still can't remember anything?"

Mark dropped his gaze and shook his head. "No. Nothing significant anyway. I get little flashes of memory but they're just fragments. None of it makes sense." He leaned back against the couch and rubbed his face. "This is so frustrating. The memories are so close I can almost touch them, but I can't quite reach."

"Give it time," Amy said gently. "Time heals all wounds, or so they say."

"Time? How much time do I have? You're a wonderful girl, Amy, for taking me in like this. I'll never be able to thank you properly. But I can't stay here forever, can I? What if I never remember?" He kept his eyes averted.

"You'll remember eventually. I'm sure of it. And you can stay here for as long as you need to."

"But..."

"Mark. It makes me feel good to be able to help you. Let me have this, okay?"

"I..."

His voice trailed off but she could read it in his eyes. His pride didn't want to impose on her, but he couldn't deny that he needed help and a safe place to stay. He needed a friend, too. And she was offering to open both her home and her life to him as a gift. He didn't quite know how to respond to her.

Mark finally looked up at her. "Thanks," was all he said.

"You look exhausted. Why don't you go back to bed?"

"I feel exhausted, but my whole body aches and I can't sleep. I thought if I got up and moved around a bit, had a hot shower, it might help my muscles relax, but every time I stand up I start to feel dizzy."

"That's because half your blood supply is probably still in that wrecked car of yours." Amy got up, grabbed his pillow from the bed, and put it on the end of the couch. Taking him by the shoulders, she gently forced him to lie down where he was.

"I have no idea exactly how much blood you lost in that car before you wrenched yourself free, but it was a lot. If you were in a real hospital they probably would have given you a blood transfusion by now. Here, you'll just have to wait until your body makes enough new blood to get your strength back. It may take awhile. I'll go get you some muscle relaxants and a pain pill from the clinic. That should help you sleep. Okay?"

"Yes, boss." He smiled, eyes half closed.

* * *

Mark was driving again. He was trying to catch up to that couple, the tall man and the beautiful woman. He kept seeing them, in the distance, around a corner, everywhere. They were watching him again, but every time he tried to drive up to them, they disappeared.

Mark's frustration built. He had to ask them. They knew.

He finally saw them standing near the doorway to an old pub off a back alley. As he drove up they looked right at him, then opened the door and slipped inside.

Now I have you! He came to a screeching halt by the door and leapt from the car. Mark burst into the pub and stopped in confusion. The place was packed. Faceless bodies milled everywhere. Cigarette smoke drifted hazily in the red glow and strobe lights flashed on and off, on and off, making everyone's movements seem choppy and segmented. Music pulsed in rhythm with the lights.

Mark scanned the room but couldn't see the couple anywhere. They had to be here. They had to! He started pushing his way through the crowd, shoving people aside, searching, searching. Where were they? He saw movement ahead. Someone was pushing through the crowd. He strained forward. The crowd parted. A tall thin man walked up to him. He had lanky hair and a scar running across his cheek. His eyes were dull and hard.

"We've been waiting for you," the scarred man said.

"You have?"

"'Course. You're one of us." He smiled a leering, twisted smile. "Follow me." He turned and disappeared into the crowd.

Mark followed, pushing and shoving, trying to catch up. "Wait! Who are you? Wait!"

Mark saw him pause up ahead, near another door. The lights and the music pulsed as one, louder and louder. The scarred man looked back, leering, and then slipped through the door. Mark clawed his way frantically past the people until he reached the door, too. He wrenched it open and burst through, tripping as he went, and crashing with a wet splat to the floor.

Everything was silent, cloaked in a dark red haze. The smell of blood filled his nose. Mark blinked, trying to clear his eyes but something blurred his vision. He pushed himself to his knees and wiped at his face.

He tasted blood. He blinked a few more times. As his vision slowly cleared, he saw his hands. They dripped red. He knelt in a pool of blood, was covered in it. Mark stared in horror as his heart began to pound. There before him a man lay, staring back at him with dead eyes, his mouth agape, a bullet hole in his forehead. The pool of blood spread wider.

Mark raised his eyes. The scarred man stood not far away. He was leaning against the wall, grinning ghoulishly. Mark sat immobilized. "Wha- what am I doing here? Who am I?" he yelled.

"I already told you.... You're one of us," the scarred man said as he began to laugh.

Mark tried to move but couldn't. He gasped for air, couldn't breathe. Everywhere he looked there were bodies and more bodies, corpse after corpse, men, women, all with dead gaping eyes. The blood spread, swelled. Then he saw them, the beautiful couple, slumped together, their eyes lifeless. The laughter rose to a crescendo. "You're one of us!"

Mark arched back and screamed,
"NO!!"

Mark jolted awake as he yelled, sending a shock-wave of pain lancing through his leg. He was lying on his back, chest heaving as he tried to catch his breath. He looked around the room frantically, then at his hands. Clean. All clean. He closed his eyes in relief. He still lay on Amy's couch.

"Mark? Did you call me?" Amy yelled from upstairs.

"N-no," he called back. "It was just the TV." He hastily grabbed the remote and flicked it on before she could come back downstairs. He stared at the TV, but all he could see were his hands soaked in blood.

Chapter Eleven

After supper, Amy and Mark had been watching TV again when headlights lit up the kitchen and Bella's barking announced the arrival of Sheriff Johnston. Amy got up to answer the knock. Mark's demeanor was markedly different by the time she came back in with Dale. Her houseguest had been relaxed and chatting with her. Now he sat stiff and tense, his face expressionless.

"Well, you're a bit of a mystery, ain't you?" Dale wasted no time announcing.

"What's that supposed to mean?" Mark countered.

"You want specifics? There's no one fitting your description on the missing persons' list for one. Your picture doesn't match anything in the data banks I have on file for criminals, military or police. Plus, we couldn't find a wallet or cell phone or any documentation at all in that car of yours."

Amy breathed a sigh of relief. He wasn't a known criminal then.

"Then there's the car itself," Dale continued. "The VIN has been filed off so I can't trace the ownership of it. The license plates are registered to an anonymous numbered company out of state. I'm working on finding out who owns it but it may take awhile. I also found a handgun in the car. It's unregistered, too. Got any explanation for that, *Mark*?"

Mark swallowed. "No. Honestly, I don't remember anything." He glanced at Amy as she chewed on her lip.

"Well, that's just real convenient, isn't it?" Dale growled. "Owning an unregistered handgun is a criminal offense."

"Slow down, Dale," Amy jumped in. "You don't even know if the gun is his."

"It was in his car!"

"It was in a car he was driving. We don't know if he owns that car. Someone else may have left the gun in there. It may not be his at all."

"Yeah, maybe the Easter Bunny owns it. Amy, he shouldn't be here. I can keep him safe down at the lock-up."

Amy saw Mark tense even further. "No, you can't Dale. You can't be there twenty-four seven and you know it. Let him stay here. I'll be fine."

"Look, Amy. There's something funny going on here and there's no evidence yet to support his 'someone's trying to kill me' story. I need to take him downtown."

"That's my story, not his. Besides, what about the car? Do you know what caused the accident yet?"

"Well, no. Trevor down at the garage won't be able to have a look at it 'til Monday or Tuesday at the earliest. But.."

"And what about those two creepy guys who have been hanging around town the last few days. Maybe they're the ones trying to kill him!"

"What two creepy guys? What are you talking about?"

"I saw them this morning in town. Christine said that they've been hanging out at the diner for a couple of days now."

* * *

As Amy began to describe the two men, the perpetual knot in Mark's gut tightened, painfully. He sat on the couch, arms folded across his chest, just staring at some imaginary spot on the floor, desperately hoping his face didn't reveal the turmoil of his thoughts.

The greasy-haired man with the scar sounded just like the one in his dream. How could that be unless he knew him? Should he tell Dale? And say what, exactly? The man in his dream had said Mark was one of them. What did that mean? He remembered the blood, the bodies, and struggled to keep his breathing even. What was he involved in? Anything? Or was it only a stupid dream? Had he hurt people? Should he just turn himself in with no memory of what he'd done, no ability to explain himself or justify his actions?

He couldn't say anything yet. It was all too nebulous. Best keep his mouth shut until he had more to go on than nightmares and conjecture. He forced his mind back to Amy's voice.

"No one knows who they are. Maybe you should check them out first," Amy finished.

Dale scowled at Amy, then at Mark, suspicion etched on his face.

* * *

Amy looked at Dale with pleading eyes. She took him by the arm and led him out to the kitchen where she spoke in hushed tones. "Please, Dale. He's okay. I have a good feeling about him. He's not going to hurt me."

"You have a good feeling, do ya? Remember the last time you had a 'good feeling'. Remember David?"

"This is different." Amy's eyes hardened at the mention of David. "I'm not in love with Mark."

"No?" Dale's voice implied he thought otherwise.

"No..." Amy tried to sound convincing but she wasn't quite sure which of them she was trying to convince more.

"Dale, please. Just wait until you check the car. See if it was sabotaged. Please?"

Dale regarded her for a long moment, then reluctantly capitulated. "Oh, all right! But I want a set of fingerprints. And I'm warning you, Amy. If he hurts you I'll shoot him dead on the spot."

Mark submitted to being fingerprinted. He sat rigidly wiping the ink from his fingers as Dale left the room. Not until Dale's car started up and drove away did he exhale loudly, slump forward and rest his head in his hands.

"It just keeps getting better and better," he said shakily, sarcasm dripping from his voice.

"It will be okay." Amy sat beside him on the couch. "God is looking after you."

"God?" Mark sat up and looked at her incredulously. "God's looking after me?

"Well, He's sure doing a bang up job so far. He's let me wreck my car, smash myself up badly, lose my memory. People are trying to kill me. Nobody nice seems to be looking for me, and I may go to jail over a gun I don't remember! Oh yeah, God's looking after me just great!"

Amy glared back at Mark. "Of course God is looking after you. That car wreck wasn't God's fault. That was caused by whoever's trying to kill you. People you became involved with. You chose bad associates and placed yourself in a dangerous situation somehow. Don't blame

God for trouble you've brought down upon your own head through bad choices."

Mark glowered at her.

Amy plowed on, her voice softer now, yet insistent. "God is the one who put trees in the path of your car so it didn't go right off the cliff. A few feet either way and there would have been nothing left of you to rescue. God is the one who kept your injuries minor. You're bruised and cut. You've lost some blood and feel weak. All that will heal in time. You could have been crippled for life, but you weren't.

"And God sent me to help you," she added, fire in her eyes.

"God sent you?" Mark snorted. "It's just a coincidence that you were the one who found me. Nothing more."

"Think about that for a moment. What are the odds that the one person who could help you, the one person in a hundred miles who had the knowledge, skill, equipment and facility to help you without going to a hospital, is the one person who did find you? Can you honestly think that's just a fluke?

"I know it was no coincidence. What are the chances that you would crash exactly where I could see you from my kitchen window? Something compelled me to go check it out. Someone. God. Believe what you want. I know the truth. God loves you, Mark, and he wants to help you. You just have to let Him."

Amy stood up and continued in a gentler tone. "I'm going to bed now. Do you need anything before I go?"

"No," he answered in a subdued tone. "And, um, thanks... for what you said to Dale...about letting me stay here."

"You're welcome." Amy smiled softly and turned to go. "Good night."

* * *

Mark watched as she made her way upstairs. He bit back the urge to call after her, to ask her to stay with him awhile longer. There was an uncomfortable emptiness pressing down upon him, and a dread of what sleep might bring. Her presence might be enough to push it back, but he feared he'd offended her with his denunciation of God.

She'd made it sound almost plausible. Could she possibly be right? Could there actually be a God who cared enough about him to try to help him? It would be nice if it was true, but he doubted it. "Even if there were a God out there," he mused aloud, "if my dreams are true, He wouldn't want anything to do with someone like me."

Mark shivered.

Earlier that day Amy had dug out an old pair of crutches from the back of a closet for him to use. He used them now to make his way to the bathroom. He'd only intended to brush his teeth, but one look at his almost beard convinced him to summon up the energy to shave. That done, he made his way back to his bed, slipped off the sweat pants, and crawled under the covers.

Lying in bed, Mark still felt cold. He pulled the blankets up a bit higher. Who was he? He'd been here for days. Why had no one reported him missing? Was there no one in his life who'd notice if he was gone? No one who'd bother to look for him? He stared up at the ceiling with knots in his stomach.

Why was there an unregistered gun in his car? It was his car. He was pretty sure of that. Amy had just been clutching at straws, trying to buy him some time, suggesting the car wasn't his. They all knew that.

And what about the guy in his dream showing up in town? Was that just sheer coincidence or reason to fear? Mark rolled carefully to his side and curled up with the blankets tucked around him.

Then there was Amy to consider. Why was she standing by him when it looked like he was nothing but trouble? Was it really because God had asked her to? That was just crazy, but when she explained things from her perspective, it sounded even crazier to believe it was all a coincidence. Mark rolled it back and forth in his mind.

* * *

Up in her own room, Amy knelt by her bed asking God some of the same questions. Who was he? What was going on with the car and the gun? Why was no one looking for him? Who was trying to kill him and why? Most importantly, why did she still believe he was a good person in spite of all the mystery?

Dale couldn't possibly be right with his insinuations that she was falling for him just like she had David. This was totally different, she assured herself. She had been young and naive with David, just a schoolgirl with a superstar boyfriend. She was older now and much wiser. She knew the danger of loving someone who wasn't what they appeared to be. She couldn't even begin to trust anyone without knowing them completely, and that disqualified Mark with his mysterious past. Yet somehow, she wanted to trust him. She couldn't explain it.

It certainly wasn't love though. She was just helping someone in need. She was being the friend she'd needed herself so many years ago, nothing more.

After praying, Amy slipped between the sheets of her bed. She didn't know how this would all work out but she clung to the belief that it would, in the end, work out. With her faith as a soothing balm, she drifted off to sleep with Franz curled up at her feet.

* * *

Downstairs Mark was tormented by memories which eluded him. Dark shadows danced just beyond his grasp. Sinister images, threatening, loomed. The more he tried to remember, the more frustrated he became.

The questions of his past haunted him. What if he didn't like what he remembered? Was he putting Amy in danger by being here? Maybe Dale should have hauled his butt off to jail just to keep her safe.

He tossed and turned in bed, every movement shooting pain through his damaged leg. He didn't care. It was a distraction from the turmoil in his mind. Finally exhaustion overcame him and he slept fitfully, plagued by nightmarish images until the morning.

* * *

When Amy came down the next morning she found Mark sitting on the couch, already dressed, absently scratching Bella's ears. She noticed he'd shaved but it hadn't improved his appearance much. There were dark circles under his eyes and tiredness etched lines into his face. The bruise on his forehead was draining down the side of his cheek, spreading in murky hues of blue, purple, and green. He turned to watch her as she crossed the room towards him.

"You look awful," she said, sympathetically. "What's wrong?"

"Couldn't sleep," he mumbled, rubbing his face.

"Was it that awful blow-up bed or Dale's cheerful info that kept you up?" she asked astutely.

"Maybe a little of both," he replied and grimaced slightly. "How is it you seem to be able to read me like a book? Am I that obvious?"

Amy just shrugged. "There's a spare room upstairs with a much more comfortable bed in it," she added. "If you think you're able to manage the stairs with those crutches we could move you in there. Then you could have some privacy when you're tired of hanging out down here. What do you think?"

"I think," Mark offered with a lopsided smile, "that you're the most thoughtful person I know."

"Hmph. Right now I'm practically the only person you know. I'll go make some coffee. It'll make you feel better.'"

Amy let Mark go up first, following behind him in case he lost his balance with the crutches. She was pleased to see that, aside from going slowly, he had no trouble at all. At the top of the stairs she led him to a sunny room with a big window facing the valley below. It was simply furnished with a double bed, a dresser, a chair and a desk. The curtains matched the blue and gold geometric pattern of the quilt. The chair was old but well padded and comfortable.

"What do you think?" Amy asked.

"Nice!" Mark sat down on the side of the bed. "Much nicer than the blow-up bed, definitely."

"Don't be ungrateful now," she said in mock reproach. "The blow-up bed was the best I could do with you unconscious. You're not exactly light you know."

"Me? Ungrateful? Never."

"I'll go get your clothes."

Amy went back downstairs and began gathering up the few clothes she had bought him. She was almost ready to go back upstairs when the phone rang.

"Hello." She answered softly, expecting it to be her mother wondering why she hadn't been in church that morning. She was prepared to pretend a headache again as her excuse for not being there. She was blind-sided by the sultry male voice which spoke instead.

"Hello, Amy. It's been a long time."

Chapter Twelve

"David?" Amy's voice rose slightly as her mind began to race. Why was he calling, now, after all this time?

"That's right, sweetheart. How've you been?"

Amy felt her teeth clench at his use of the word 'sweetheart'. "That's kind of a loaded question, don't you think, since the last time we spoke I was in the hospital and we were still a couple?"

"Are you still mad about that, sweetheart? That was a long time ago. I was hoping we could get together for drinks or something, maybe at your place." His voice dripped with charm.

"Are you crazy? You can't just waltz back into my life and pick up where we left off. Not after all this time."

"Come on, darling. Don't you remember how it was between us? It could be that way again. I miss those incredible green eyes of yours. They always used to drive me wild."

Amy could picture him in her mind's eye. He stood tall and straight, a consummate athlete. He had the face of a model, finely molded, with flawless skin and perfect teeth, framed by ultra-blonde wavy hair. His eyes were icy blue, like a winter sky. She'd always thought of them as beautiful before. Now, as she remembered them, they just seemed cold.

"Forget it." Amy's voice shook. "I'm not the same naive little girl anymore. You can't suck me in with all that charm the way you used to. If you're calling me now it's because you want something from me. I just can't figure out what. Whatever it is, I'm not interested."

"But, darling.."

"Stop! This conversation is over. Don't call me again."

Amy hung up the phone before he could say anything else. She sat on the couch, as a too familiar pain crushed her chest. What on earth did he want after all these years? Could he really want to rekindle their romance for love's sake? No, he'd have some hidden agenda behind his actions. David always did what was best for David. He really didn't care how that might affect anyone else, including her. That's what hurt so much.

She angrily brushed a tear off her cheek. Stupid! Stupid! Don't waste your tears on that idiot.

I need a cup of tea. Amy leaped off the couch and launched herself towards the kitchen.

She put the kettle on and began searching through her tea bags. She finally chose a soothing herbal blend and poured the water into her teapot, slowly beginning to calm down as she waited for it to steep. Her reaction didn't surprise her. So many years had passed, but the scars ran deep.

"Shoot!" she whispered. She should have controlled herself long enough to find out what he really wanted before she hung up on him. Oh, well. Too late now.

Amy suddenly realized she'd forgotten about Mark upstairs. Quickly pouring him some tea also, she grabbed the cups and hurried back upstairs.

"Sorry I was gone so long. The phone rang and..." Amy stopped dead in her tracks, mouth open. Mark was standing on one leg by the open closet door reading the inscription on a trophy. The whole upper shelf was filled with similar trophies of various sizes. "What are you doing?" Her voice rose angrily, but Mark didn't notice immediately.

"I got bored waiting so I began looking around. You didn't mention you used to be a figure skater." The smile on his face froze as he noticed the cold fury on hers.

Amy strode across the room, face white, eyes glittering. She snatched the trophy from his hands and thrust it back into the closet almost slamming the door closed. "That was a long time ago and I don't want to talk about it. You have no business snooping through my house. Are you going to check out my bedroom next? Should I get a lock?"

"Of course not..."

"I don't have to tell you everything, you know. I hardly even know you. Just because I let you use this room..."

"That's right!" Mark interrupted her sharply. "You said I could use this room. Your idea, not mine. You didn't say anything about staying out of the closet. How was I supposed to know?"

Amy glared at him. The truth was she'd forgotten that stuff was in there. She'd hidden it all away years ago so she wouldn't have to think about it. Now, within the space of half an hour, all her old wounds had been ripped open. Still, he was right. She had offered the room and hadn't asked him to stay out of the closet.

"Sorry," she offered reluctantly, eyes down.

"Why are all your trophies hidden away in this closet anyway? Most people would display at least a few of them."

Amy glared at him again, stone-faced, her eyes hard. "I told you. That part of my life is over and I don't want to talk about it. Please stay out of there. I'll go get your clothes, and then I'm taking Bella for a walk." She spun on her heel and left before Mark could say anything further.

* * *

Mark sat propped up on the bed with his feet up for a long time after Amy left for her walk. What just happened? She'd been furious. Why get so riled up over a bunch of old trophies? He glanced at the closet for the umpteenth time. The urge to investigate was overpowering. If she had just casually brushed it off, he'd probably have forgotten about it by now, but her extreme reaction had his curiosity piqued.

She had asked him to stay out but he never actually agreed to do so, he reasoned. He got up and crutched over to the window. There was no sign of her. Keeping his ears peeled for any sound of the door opening, he made his way over to the closet again.

An hour later he had removed, examined, and carefully replaced every trophy on the shelf. The smaller ones were Amy's at the junior level. The larger and more recent ones were for pairs figure skating. The same two names appeared on all of them; Amy Scott and David Jansen. Some of them were from local competitions but most were at the national and international level. The most recent was just over twelve years old.

Hanging in the back corner of the closet, behind layers of large winter coats, he found several fancy skating costumes. He pulled one out, giving it a brief shake and a cloud of dust filled the air. The costume was an iridescent mix of blues, greens and silver that must have dazzled under the spotlight. The frilly little skirt was randomly dotted with sequins which would have added to the sparkle. At the moment, however, it looked rather forlorn, covered in a fine layer of dust. So, too, did a very expensive-looking pair of skates tucked neatly in the corner.

Mark put everything carefully away, closed the door firmly, and made his way back to his bed. He lay on his back, hands under his head, mulling over what he'd found in the closet.

Amy had obviously been good, very good. Why had she stopped skating? To become that good she must have been passionate about it. Even if she'd retired from competition, wouldn't she still skate just for the love of the sport? The skates in the closet looked like they hadn't been moved in many years. Something drastic had happened, obviously, but what? And who was this David Jansen fellow?

Mark had even more questions than before, but no easy way to get answers. Amy had been very clear about not wanting to talk about it. He'd just have to come up with another way to find out.

Chapter Thirteen

Amy was glad to be working in the clinic Monday morning. Her life had become so complicated over the last six days, that it was good to be back with her animal patients again. They were simple and straightforward to deal with for the most part. Their owners weren't always easy, of course, but even they were a blessing compared with the current turmoil of her own life.

She had walked for a long time with Bella the night before until the cool air and vigorous exercise had washed the anger from her system. Any mention of David or her past skating career always caused such extreme emotions within her that her friends and family had long ago learned to avoid the subject. Poor Mark, though, had had no idea what demons he was stirring up for her. Combine that with the unexpected call from David himself and it was no wonder she'd flipped out.

She'd returned from her walk after several hours and had made her way back upstairs to Mark's room to apologize for her behavior. She had found him sound asleep, flat on his back, with his hands under his head. She'd sat on the edge of the chair for a moment, hoping he might awake, but he hadn't. Disappointed, she'd draped a blanket over him and left him to sleep.

Remembering now, Amy breathed a sigh of relief that he had been sleeping. In the mood she was in last night, she might have confessed all her secrets to him and that would never do. You just don't bare your soul to someone you hardly know. Who knows what they might do with the information? She wasn't ready to risk it in the bright light of day, but last night... What was it about him that made it so hard to keep her guard up?

* * *

Mark sat staring at the computer screen. He'd originally intended to try to find information on missing persons, hoping to find himself there, but somehow he'd Googled Amy Scott instead. It made for an interesting read.

She'd started figure skating at age ten and, according to the articles, had shown great promise even then. By age fifteen she was a contender in pairs figure skating and by seventeen she was partnered with David Jansen, the best male skater in the state. Together, they had been almost unbeatable.

Mark studied the picture of the two of them together, posing on the ice. A much younger Amy wore that same iridescent blue-green outfit he'd seen in the closet the night before. It glistened in the light, clinging to her body and accentuating every curve of her tiny frame. She had one arm raised, as if she were a rare tropical bird about to take flight. David stood beside her, tall, blonde, and handsome in a matching outfit.

Mark scowled at the image before him, an uncomfortable feeling beginning to build in his gut. Amy clung to David, gazing up at him with adoration in her eyes. A beautiful smile lit her face, and it was all for him. David, however, smiled at the camera with arrogance, a haughty expression on his face. He paid no more attention to her than if she was some trophy he'd just won. She was obviously in love. He was just as obviously in love with only himself.

As he gazed at Amy's expression, Mark's jaw clenched. He'd only seen her smile like that once, when he'd first awakened in her home. She'd been so relieved and so caught off guard that her expression had been pure and uninhibited joy. She had smiled since then, of course, but it was always somewhat constrained. There was joy and passion within her, Mark could sense it, yet she rarely let it peek out.

Mark found himself wishing she would look at him with that same expression she'd bestowed on David. Thinking about her and David was causing that uncomfortable, possessive knot in his stomach to grow. It was beginning to feel a little like jealousy, he noted, somewhat surprised at himself.

Mark sat up straighter and began reading further. Amy and David had blown away the local competition and had gone on to be serious contenders at the national and international level. They had taken second place at the Worlds that year and had been favored to take a medal at the upcoming Olympics. It seemed the world was their oyster and it was only going to get better.

A search of the Olympic records that year, however, showed no Amy Scott listed anywhere as a competitor. When he searched David's name, Mark found he'd placed way down the list with some other woman as his partner. What had happened?

Further investigation finally turned up the missing piece of the puzzle. Mark read the article in dismay.

"Local figure skater and Olympic hopeful, Amy Scott, was seriously injured last night when the vehicle she was riding in was T-boned by a pick-up truck on Highway 90. Scott was rushed to the hospital with multiple fractures and internal bleeding. She is now listed in serious but stable condition.

"Doctors believe Scott will likely make a full recovery given time, but say it is unlikely she will be ready to attend this year's Olympics which commence in only five months. Some have questioned whether she will ever be able to skate at a professional level again.

"The cause of the crash remains under investigation."

Mark leaned back in his chair, still staring at the screen in front of him. So that's why everything to do with skating was hidden in the spare room closet. From the looks of things, she hadn't skated since the accident over twelve years ago. Obviously, the memories were still very painful to her. Was there more to it than just the loss of her skating career though? Mark guessed there was, and he was willing to bet David had something to do with it.

* * *

Over the next few days Amy and Mark developed a bit of a routine. Amy went to work in the clinic each day while Mark quietly watched TV, read books, or surfed the Net when he wasn't just catching up on his sleep. Amy would join him for lunch and they would spend the evenings together, sometimes watching TV but more often talking while playing cards or Scrabble.

She told him stories from her childhood, growing up with her parents and her older sister, Carmen. She also had plenty of stories from her years at university studying to be a vet. There were no stories at all, however, involving skating. Mercifully for Amy, Mark never brought it up.

She could see the questions in his eyes sometimes, burning to be asked. A lump of anxiety would suddenly form in the pit of her stomach as she'd brace herself for the interrogation she was sure was coming, but then he would drop his eyes, smile, look back at her and change the subject. She didn't know whether to feel relieved or disappointed.

Part of her wished he would ask, push her just a little. She liked him so much, and the trusting, lonely side of her nature wanted to finally share her pain with someone. Then the wounded, frightened Amy would start calling herself stupid, foolish and naive. You can't trust someone you don't know and you can't possibly know someone who can't even remember his own name. Haven't you learned anything?

Mark, however, never pushed the issue. Slowly, in spite of herself, Amy began to relax more and more in his presence. Instead of dreading the end of the day with its long, lonely evenings of TV reruns, she found herself anxiously awaiting her time with him. Somehow, he always managed to make her laugh, usually within a few minutes of being together. He never seemed to tire of hearing her stories and, though he had no stories of his own to tell, he always had strong opinions about whatever she'd shared with him.

On top of that was the undeniable physical attraction. Amy's pulse would begin to race before she even got through the door at the end of the day. She tried to tell herself not to be foolish, but herself didn't pay attention too well. Amy tried to keep a respectable distance between them, but every so often he would brush her arm accidentally or touch her briefly with his hand. That would be enough to make her whole body heat up.

Mark was always a gentleman. Though he did openly flirt with her regularly, it was mostly done in a light, teasing manner which never left her feeling uncomfortable. Occasionally, she would turn unexpectedly and catch him staring at her, his blue eyes deep and fathomless. Their eyes would meet briefly, and Amy would feel as if she'd just been jolted with electricity. Then Mark would wink at her, she would laugh and the moment would be gone.

Thursday evening began in their usual way. Amy finished clearing up the supper dishes and returned to the living room where Mark sat on the couch running his fingertips up and down Franz's back causing all the hair to stand up at odd angles. The cat's hind feet were planted firmly on the floor while his forearms rested in Mark's lap and he arched backwards in feline pleasure, eyes half closed, a soft smile curling his furry lips. Amy paused to watch a moment, feeling a warm sense of contentment at the comfy scene before her. It almost felt like... a family.

Amy gulped uncomfortably. She shouldn't even think things like that. This wasn't going to last. No point in entertaining unrealistic fantasies. She shook her head abruptly, as if to dislodge the futile dreams trying to form there.

The movement must have caught Mark's attention because he glanced up at her, still scratching the cat.

"Hey. What's up?"

"I… I should check the stitches on your leg" she said, grasping at an excuse to be standing there, staring at him.

"They were fine this morning when I had a shower."

"I'm sure they were. Still, I should check," she insisted.

With a resigned look Mark pushed the cat gently aside, lay down and slid his sweat pants down off his hips to reveal the bandage taped securely to his leg. Amy peeled the tape off carefully to expose the long line of staples running down his thigh. She examined them closely, prodding gently with her fingertips to check for infection and to gauge how well the flesh was knitting back together.

She tried to ignore how incredibly good he smelled at the moment. He was wearing that aftershave she'd bought and, while it wasn't really noticeable from a few feet away, up close it was almost intoxicating. He smelled warm and exciting and, well, delicious. The way he was looking at her didn't help either. He was lying with his head in his hand, watching her with hooded eyes, a faint smile tugging at the corners of his mouth as if he could sense her response. The air seemed to tingle between them, or maybe, Amy thought, it was just her that was tingling.

Amy cleared her throat. "Okay, um, I need you to bend your knee please. A bit further, please."

Mark's wince was barely perceptible as he slowly bent the leg. Amy watched closely. The skin held securely and the muscles all seemed to stay in place beneath the skin.

"Good. Now straighten it again,"

A cold sweat had broken out on Mark's brow as he complied with her request.

"Sorry about that," she said ruefully, "but I need to be sure the muscles are connected properly or your leg will never be normal."

"Don't worry about me. I'm fine," Mark's voice rasped, his face pale.

"Liar."

He smiled slightly at that, then rested his head down and closed his eyes while Amy applied some more ointment and re-bandaged the leg.

Amy let out a guilty sigh. At least he wasn't making eyes at her anymore. It seemed impossible to think straight when she got this close to him and he looked at her that way. She hadn't felt this way about anyone since... David.

Amy swallowed hard. No. She couldn't possibly be falling for Mark. She didn't know a thing about him, not even his real name. No, absolutely not. She was lonely and it was nice to have someone around to talk to, that's all. Sure he was sexy, so what? With a handsome guy like him there was bound to be some base attraction. She didn't have to obey her instincts like some kind of wild animal though.

The ring of the telephone interrupted her thoughts. She crossed the room to answer it while Mark hiked his pants back up.

"That was Dale. He's coming over."

Chapter Fourteen

Mark's smile froze on his face, and then faded. He sat up a little straighter on the couch and tried to assume a relaxed pose. Amy wasn't fooled. She'd been getting to know him quite well over the past few days. Even though he looked relaxed outwardly, she could feel the tension radiating from him. She was suddenly anxious, too, and a large knot formed in the pit of her stomach to prove it.

Amy jumped when Dale pounded on the door only minutes later. He let himself in before she could even get there to answer it.

"That was fast. You just called a minute ago," Amy remarked.

"Yeah, well, I was already on my way here when I called," Dale said gruffly, striding into the living room.

"He didn't want me to slip out the back door before he could get here," Mark interjected emotionlessly. He met Dale's eyes directly as the older man gave him a narrow, appraising look.

Dale continued, after a poignant pause, as if Mark hadn't spoken. "I just finished talking with Trevor, down at the garage." He tossed a photo onto the coffee table in front of Mark. "That's a picture of your brake line, or what's left of it."

Amy moved to sit beside Mark as he examined the photo. She was so intrigued by the evidence that she didn't notice Dale's scowl at the sight of her sitting thigh to thigh next to Mark. They both looked up in unison as Dale cleared his throat loudly.

"Trevor tells me it was a clever job. Someone cut back the rubber coating on the brake line and then used some kind of file, probably a Dremel, to grind down a large section of the metal liner until it was paper thin. If they'd just cut the line, your brakes would have given out slowly. You'd have noticed the loss of power before ever having an accident. This way, you'd have had full brakes as long as you used them gently, but the moment you needed to stop fast and stomped on them hard, that whole chunk of line would blow out at once. You'd have lost your brakes instantly." He paused a moment, then added, "Trevor found both sides blown out and brake fluid splattered all over everything. You should be dead, boy."

Amy looked sharply at Mark, flashing her best 'I told you so' expression. Mark remained focused on the picture in his hands as Dale continued speaking.

"So, mystery-boy here was right about someone trying to do him in. The big question now is, who'd want to kill such a fine, upstanding young man as Mark here?"

Sarcasm edged his voice. "Is your memory still conveniently absent?"

"This is hardly convenient!" Mark snapped. "Hiding here while someone's stalking me. If I knew who they were don't you think I'd tell you? If I knew *anything*, why wouldn't I tell you?" The face from his dream thrust itself to the front of his mind but Mark shoved it ruthlessly back. That was just a dream, not reality. It meant nothing. He hoped.

"'Cause maybe," Dale said, pausing for effect, "you'd be implicating yourself just as much as them. And maybe you're having too much fun playing house with Amy here!"

Mark shoved himself to his feet to meet Dale eye to eye. "I'm not lying and I don't like what you're implying," he said through gritted teeth. From standing, he had a height advantage of several inches which he used to stare down at Dale. His hands clenched reflexively but he made no move to touch the sheriff.

Dale stood his ground, unflinching. His hand rested casually upon the holster at his hip. His eyes flashed a warning and his chin jutted out as if daring Mark to try something stupid.

In a second, Amy jumped between them, placing a gentle hand on each man's chest. Glaring at each man alternately, willing them to calm down, she said, "Please, stop. This isn't helping. Can't you two co-operate?"

Neither man moved for a long moment. Mark eased back slightly. Placing his hand protectively over hers, which still rested against his chest, he turned his attention towards her, saying, "Maybe we could all use a nice cup of coffee. Would you please go make some?"

Amy met his eyes. He seemed calmer and more in control of himself. She looked back at Dale. He'd removed his hand from his gun and now stood with arms crossed in front of him, still watching Mark carefully. Dale gestured with his head towards the kitchen, indicating she should go. Amy glared at him but finally capitulated and turned towards the kitchen.

* * *

Mark let her hand slip from his grasp as she left, and turned his attention back towards Dale. Once she was out of hearing range, he quietly continued, "Look, I know this all seems pretty suspicious but I honestly can't remember. I wish I could tell you who is after me and why. If I knew who to call, or where I could go to be safe, I'd leave right now."

"You would, would ya? Just like that?" Dale sounded skeptical. Leaning in towards Mark, Dale fixed him with a steely glare and said, "You look me straight in the eye, boy, and tell me you ain't enjoying yourself just the tiniest little bit, being holed up here alone with Amy."

Mark averted his eyes for the briefest second and didn't answer. Guilty as accused.

Dale leaned back a bit and gloated, "Thought so. You like her, don't ya?"

Mark felt like squirming but met Dale's stare directly. "Yeah. So what? All the more reason to believe me. I don't want to see her get hurt. If I knew anything that would help, I'd tell you."

Mark sighed and dropped back down on the couch. He winced as a stab of pain shot through his leg. Leaning his head back on the couch he continued, "My just being here probably puts her in danger. We should find somewhere else for me to be. Right now."

Dale regarded Mark for several long moments. "Yeah, I'd already considered that. Decided against it."

Mark looked up at Dale, not quite believing his ears. "Why?"

"Well, where else am I going to put you? This is a small town. People talk. They can't help themselves. If I move you to anywhere else around here, the whole bloody town will know about you within twenty-four hours."

"What about moving me to another town?"

"Not a chance! This is attempted murder we're talking about here. Not only are you the intended victim but you're also the only witness, if you can ever remember anything. No. You're staying right here in my jurisdiction. Besides, whoever did this won't know for sure where you crashed. They'll be watching all the neighboring towns for you, too."

"What about Amy?"

"As long as no one knows you're here, you'll both be safe. The people responsible can't exactly go door to door looking for you. It would draw too much attention to them. No, they have to sit back and hope you're dumb enough to show yourself. You ain't that dumb, are you, boy?"

"No." Mark glared at Dale until he noticed the twinkle in the older man's eye. He was just about to relax a little when Dale leaned in towards him again, his face stern.

"Just one more thing," he said ominously. "You seem like a decent enough fellow on the surface, but I still don't know who the hell you are or what you've done that's got people after you, and until I do, you don't have my permission to cozy up with Amy."

"You're *permission*?" Mark countered, incredulously.

"That's right. My permission. When Amy's father died years ago, I promised her mom I'd keep an eye on her, and that's what I'm doing. So, you'd best keep your hands to yourself or I'll change my mind about you staying here and move you to a nice safe jail cell!"

"Doesn't Amy have any say in this?" Mark grumbled.

"No, she don't. This is between you and me. Besides, that girl's skittish as a spring filly when it comes to men. I doubt you'd stand a chance anyway."

Mark's back stiffened at the jibe. He was about to tell Dale where to go when Amy's voice startled them both.

"Stand a chance at what?" She stood before them, holding a tray with coffee cups and some sort of sliced cake, eyeing them suspiciously.

"Uh..." Mark began.

"Nothing important, sweetheart," Dale jumped in. "Oh, good. You've brought the coffee. And what's this?" He grabbed a slice of cake, smiling broadly.

"Banana bread." She glanced suspiciously between the two of them.

"I was just telling Mark that the fingerprints may take awhile to get back. The system's backlogged right now. We won't stand a chance of getting the results in less than a couple of weeks." Dale was still smiling a little too much.

Amy scowled slightly. Mark held his breath. Would she buy that story? Only a few minutes ago Dale had been ready to shoot him and now he was grinning like they were buds. She glanced suspiciously between them, obviously not convinced.

"Anyway," Dale continued, "the bottom line is, Mark was right about his car being sabotaged, so he'll have to stay hidden here until he either gets his memory back, or I can find out what's going on some other way. I'm still working on the other lines of investigation but they'll take awhile."

Dale grabbed another piece of banana bread and started heading for the door. He stopped and turned back towards Amy. "Oh, and I checked out those two strangers you were worried about in town. Apparently they're associates of David's." He paused. "Did you know he was back in town?"

"Yes," Amy said flatly. "He called earlier this week. He wanted to come over for drinks."

Mark sat up straighter, his attention instantly riveted to her. He quickly searched her face. Did she still love him? He held his breath as he waited for her to continue.

Dale's eyes narrowed. "What'd you say?"

"I said 'no'," she admitted. "But I did wonder what he wanted. Maybe I should have said yes. Just to find out."

Mark exhaled slowly. She'd said 'no'. That was good. He relaxed back onto the couch.

Amy followed Dale to the door to see him out while Mark watched discreetly.

In spite of the disturbing news that his car really had been sabotaged, he struggled to hide the smile which threatened to break out on his face. He found himself ridiculously pleased at Amy's refusal to see David.

Still, hearing that David was trying to get back into her life had caused that possessive little knot in his stomach to reassert itself. And she'd suggested seeing him, so maybe there was still something between them. His smile faded a fraction.

There was something else, too. Something about David was tugging at the back of his mind, but try as he might, he just couldn't remember.

Chapter Fifteen

Mark stood in a dark alley, under the misty glow of a street light. There were two men with him, one tall and lanky with stringy hair and a scar across his cheek, the other shorter and thick-set with dark hair, little piggy eyes, and wearing a black leather jacket. They were waiting.

Mist drifted up from the ground like spirits rising from their graves. A chill breeze made them dance and swirl in the lamplight. Mark shivered. Somewhere, water dripped into a puddle.

They waited.

Something moved down at the far end of the alley. He heard footsteps, voices, echoing off the damp concrete walls. The dark-haired man nudged Mark. He was holding a gun, offering it. Mark saw the gun, saw his own hand reach out and take it. He raised the gun and pointed it down the alley.

His mind screamed, 'RUN! GET AWAY! RUN NOW!'

He said nothing.

He fired. Once. Twice. The voices stopped. Water dripped.

The three of them walked down the alley, chatting, joking. There was something on the ground up ahead. Mark wanted to stop, turn back, run away.

He kept moving forwards.

They stopped in front of two bodies on the ground, a man and a woman. The man lay on his back, sprawled awkwardly, his face obscured by the hair of the woman who lay face down on top of him. Mark's companions were laughing. Mark was laughing, too. He didn't want to look, didn't want to see their faces. He reached down, grabbed the woman by her shoulder and flipped her over. Dark curly hair framed a graceful face. Dead blue eyes stared back at him. It was them. The beautiful couple.

Mark was laughing. Water blurred his vision.

Suddenly, he was sitting in a back booth of a pub. All around him, people milled, laughing, as the music pulsed. Cigarette haze drifted around in the dim red lighting. The scarred man sat on his right, the dark one on his left. They were laughing and drinking. Mark laughed with them as fear clawed at his insides. His pulse raced. It was hard to breathe.

Mark's hand rested around a glass of amber liquid on the table. He lifted the glass and swallowed deeply, feeling the burn snake down his throat. The warmth calmed him.

"They knew me. They could have told me who I am," Mark said coldly, all traces of laughter gone.

"We know who you are, too, don't we?" the scarred man replied, leering and raising his glass.

The dark-haired man grinned in response and clinked glasses with the other, as they both began laughing again.

Mark looked back and forth between them. "Who am I? Tell me!"

"You?" the dark-haired man said malevolently, his smile twisting into a snarl. He withdrew a gun from inside his jacket and touched the barrel to Mark's forehead. "You're a dead man."

He squeezed the trigger.

Mark bolted upright with a gasp, his heart hammering in his chest, his body soaked in sweat. He sat for a moment, trembling, his breath coming in ragged sobs as the adrenaline still coursed through his veins. He slowly eased himself back down onto the bed and lay there, staring at the ceiling as the early dawn light began to seep through the curtains. It was just a dream. Just a dream.

* * *

Amy stroked the old cat's head gently before handing her back to the elderly lady in her examination room. "Sadie is doing much better, Mrs. McCormick. I've injected some fluid under her skin to re-hydrate her, but she'll probably need to come in once every week or two for more fluids to keep her healthy."

"But she will be okay, won't she?" Mrs. McCormick said with a worried little frown. "She's very dear to me."

"Well, with her thyroid not working properly for so long, it has caused some damage to her kidneys, but as long as we keep her on thyroid medication and keep her hydrated, she should be fine for a good long while." Amy smiled reassuringly. "Just stop by the front desk and Candace will get the medication for you."

As Mrs. McCormick took her cat away towards the small waiting area by the front desk, Amy began cleaning up the exam room. She sprayed down the exam table with disinfectant and swept up the floor. That done, she went back towards the surgery area to do a quick double-check of the medicine cabinet. Candace met her there.

"Front office's all cleaned up," she announced cheerfully. "Need any help here?"

"No, thanks. I already placed the order for supplies earlier today. I guess we're set 'til tomorrow."

"Only one more day 'til the weekend!" Candace grinned saucily. "Guess what Jason and I are doing this Saturday?"

"What?"

"We're going down to the coast and staying at this cute little B and B we found on-line."

"Sounds nice," Amy said noncommittally.

"What about you? Had any luck with the on-line dating yet?"

"Um, well, I've talked to a couple of fellows but nothing's clicked yet," Amy lied, Mark's dreamy smile hovering in the back of her mind.

She'd spent the majority of the week since Dale's last visit with Mark. His leg was healing up fairly well and the better he felt physically, the more restless he became. Amy could easily sympathize with him. She well remembered the long hours of agonizing boredom in the months following her car accident. So, she tried to spend as much time with Mark as she could, just to offer him some company other than Bella and Franz. She rented movies and they played cards or other board games, anything to pass the time. As his leg improved, they ventured into her secluded back yard to throw sticks for Bella to fetch. The only times she left him to his own devices were to go to work and then to church Sunday morning.

She tried to tell herself it was all for his benefit. She was just doing him a favor, keeping him company. In a few moments of unguarded self-honesty though, she had to admit she was enjoying herself very much. Try as she might to remain detached, just being near him made her smile and, somehow, he usually had her laughing before long. Still, not far below the surface, was a very real fear that lay ready to throw up the barricades to protect her at the least provocation.

She felt, at times, like a moth dancing around a campfire. The danger of getting burned was very real, but somehow she just couldn't resist the temptation to draw ever closer to that which she both feared and longed for.

"Oh for heaven's sake, Amy!" Candace's voice wrenched her back to the moment. "It's been nearly two weeks since you signed up and you still haven't gone on a date with anyone? I think you're just too picky. When are you going to stop hiding from life and get out there and live a little?"

"It's not that simple."

"Sure it is. You're never going to fall in love if you won't even go on a date with anyone."

"Stop worrying about me, Candace. The right guy will come along eventually."

"Really? How're you going to meet this 'right guy' if you won't date? Are you just going to pick him up off the side of the road?"

"Maybe," Amy said, coyly.

Candace rolled her eyes. "Whatever, Amy. Just don't blame me if you wind up an old lady all alone in a nursing home one day." She grabbed her purse and sauntered out the door.

Amy watched her climb into her little car and pull out of the small clinic parking area with a wave. Maybe Candace was right. She'd have to start dating sometime if she didn't want to be alone for the rest of her life. The problem right now was, she couldn't seem to think of anyone but Mark. She certainly couldn't date him.

Amy turned off the clinic lights and opened the door to her living room. As she walked in she was engulfed by the most wonderful aroma of roast beef and vegetables. She closed her eyes for a moment and just breathed in the scent.

She was immediately transported back to her childhood, and the wonderful dinners her mother had made while her father was still alive. Amy remembered coming in from the cold, and being enfolded in the warmth of home and family. Dinners had been full of laughter and stories of the day's happenings. It was a far cry from eating supper alone in front of the TV which is what she'd grown accustomed to lately, before Mark entered her life.

"Hello!" she called out tentatively.

"In here," Mark answered from the kitchen.

"What's all this?" she asked as she came into the kitchen.

Mark stood at the stove stirring what Amy assumed was gravy, but he glanced her way as she entered. "I was getting pretty bored doing nothing all day, so I decided to make dinner. Hope you don't mind."

"Not at all. It smells wonderful!" Amy said with pleasure.

Mark grinned and Amy's heart did a little flutter in her chest. He looked devastatingly handsome at the moment, dressed in jeans and a fitted black T-shirt. His dark hair lay in tousled damp waves like he'd just emerged from the shower. Amy smiled to herself at the mental image *that* thought conjured up.

Glancing down, she realized the same couldn't be said for herself. The scrub uniform she'd worn all day was looking decidedly grubby and God only knew what that stain was. Hair was starting to escape from her ponytail and Amy was sure she smelled of disinfectant. She nervously ran her hands down the front of her scrubs, as if that would somehow help. For some reason it suddenly became extremely important that she look more presentable.

"Do you need any help? Or do I have time to go freshen up?"

Mark glanced back at her again. "It's almost ready but you probably have about ten minutes if you need them."

Without a word Amy dashed upstairs, stripped off her scrubs and jumped into the shower for a quick wash. Five minutes later she had slipped on her best jeans, the stretch ones that hugged her curves flawlessly, and topped them with a clingy lightweight russet-colored sweater. She gave her hair a cursory blow-dry, leaving it still slightly damp and allowing the natural wave to manifest itself. Finally, she added a touch of eye makeup, a swish of lip gloss and a hint of her favorite scent.

Amy gave herself a final look in the mirror. The push-up bra did wonders for what little God had endowed her with. She smoothed down the front of her sweater, checked out her rear view, and took a deep breath to steady the butterflies in her tummy. Then she froze, staring at the wide-eyed, excited girl in the mirror.

What was she doing? Primping and preening like this was some kind of date? So he made dinner. So what? She'd done all the cooking since he'd arrived, so it was kind of his turn anyway. This was nothing special. It was just supper. After all, they had to eat. Taking a firmer grip on her emotions, Amy headed back down to the kitchen.

"Hey, I'm back. What can I do to help?" she announced breezily, as if her palms weren't totally sweaty.

"I'm pretty much done, but you could help me carry this food out to the sundeck..." Mark's reply trailed off as he turned towards her. He stopped abruptly, staring at her with a warm smile.

Amy felt almost naked as his eyes scanned her from head to foot and back up again. She felt an absurd little thrill of power to see him momentarily at a loss for words, and was suddenly glad she'd taken the time to lose the baggy uniform.

"It's... uh… it's so warm this evening I thought we could eat out on the deck for a change," Mark fumbled, appearing to have lost his train of thought. He handed her a platter covered in roast beef, potatoes, onions and carrots. "Everything else is already out there."

"Wow!" Amy said, trying to focus on the food. "You've gone all out."

Mark gave a self-deprecating shrug. "Like I said, I was bored." He picked up the gravy and limped towards the living room.

"Hey. Where are your crutches?"

"In the corner. It was too awkward to cook with them. I thought I'd try walking a bit. The leg's not too bad as long as I go slow."

"Just don't push it too much, hmm?"

"Yes, Mom," he replied with a wink.

Amy followed him out through the glass doors and found the porch table set and ready to go, complete with ice water, a bottle of red wine and the only two wine glasses she owned. "Where'd you find this?" she asked, indicating the wine.

"It was tucked away in the bottom of the pantry. I hope you weren't saving it for a special occasion."

"No. I must have bought it for Christmas last year and then never used it. I'd forgotten all about it."

"Good. We can drink it guilt free then."

Mark set the gravy down, then pulled out a chair for Amy to sit.

Flushing at the unaccustomed chivalry, Amy took her seat as Mark set up the wine glasses and reached for the bottle. She watched, fascinated, at the way the muscles of his forearm rippled beneath the skin as he wound the corkscrew into the cork, then twisted it open with a pop. Taking one of the glasses, he poured in a mouthful, swirled it around a couple of times, and then sniffed the glass.

"Mmm, nice bouquet." Mark flashed a smile at her and then drank the contents, holding the wine in his mouth briefly before swallowing. He considered a moment before continuing, "Full-bodied, satiny, with a smooth finish, and just a hint of pepper. This should go well with dinner."

He took the other glass and filled it before offering it to Amy. "M'Lady."

Amy accepted the wine with a laugh. Without thinking she said, "You sound like you actually know what you're talking about. Where'd you learn about wine?"

Mark opened his mouth as if to answer, then hesitated. After a moment he offered her a lopsided smile and with a shrug of his shoulders admitted, "I have no idea. I seem to come up with stuff right out of the blue, then, when I try to link it back to a memory, I just come up blank."

"Well, you obviously have some culture in your background somewhere, or you wouldn't know squat about wine. I can't imagine a street thug commenting that his wine was satiny, or whatever it was you said," Amy replied.

Mark's answering grin seemed just a little relieved as he said, "Hey. Good point. I hadn't thought of that."

Dinner was delicious. Amy savored every aspect of it, from the food and the wine, to the conversation and the ambience. Something magical tingled in the air between them and the laughter flowed.

Sparkles of light danced off the lake in the valley below. The setting sun cast a warm, orange glow on the forest surrounding the lake and her home. In the trees, birds twittered and sang echoing the happiness in Amy's heart. She sighed in contentment.

It was just like in her daydreams.

That thought brought her up cold. She'd always imagined doing this very thing with some faceless, as yet to be discovered, man. Now, the man in her daydream had a face, Mark's face, with its little scar on the brow. He had Mark's deep blue, see-straight-through-your-soul eyes and his dark unruly hair, too. Amy swallowed hard and glanced apprehensively towards him, only to find him watching her intently.

"What?" he asked softly.

"Pardon?" she replied, trying to pretend she didn't know what he meant.

"You were looking so happy there for a moment, then something changed. What just happened in your head?" His voice was gentle, persuasive.

"Nothing." Amy forced a tight smile. "This was a lovely dinner. Thank you. We should probably start cleaning up now though. It's starting to get chilly."

Amy stood and began gathering up the dishes into a pile. With two empty wine glasses in one hand and the bottle in the other, she turned to go back to the kitchen only to find Mark standing inches in front of her. Amy stopped abruptly, heart inexplicably pounding, her nose level with his chest. His cologne filled her senses, deliciously spicy with hints of amber. Desire flooded through her, and she struggled to maintain her composure.

Gently he placed one finger under her chin and tilted her face up until she had no choice but to look at him. She stood, trembling, eyes locked to his. She read desire there, and something else. Sadness?

"How long, Amy? How long are you going to keep this wall up between us?" he asked softly.

"I don't know what you're talking about," she lied, averting her eyes as he gently placed his hands on either side of her face.

"Yes, you do." He stroked her cheekbone with his thumb sending thrills of pleasure racing down her spine. "You've got this wall up around your heart. It must be at least a mile high, but every so often I see it start to fall. Then something happens and you slam it back up again."

"Yeah?" Amy countered lamely. "Well... Life is safer that way, isn't it?"

"Maybe. I'm sure you think it keeps the pain out, but it keeps the joy out, too, and I'll bet there are times you still hurt anyway."

Amy turned her face away again, scowling. How did he do that? How could he see right through her like she was made of glass? Was everything in her heart stamped out on her forehead for him to read? The worst part was, sometimes she felt like glass. One wrong move and she might shatter into a million pieces. She didn't dare let him see that.

"What would you know about it?" she replied defensively. "You don't even know your own name."

She regretted the words as soon as they left her mouth but he ignored her waspishness. Smiling, he ran his fingers up through her hair and turned her face back towards him again.

"I know there's a smart, gutsy, passionate woman trapped inside you just begging to come out," he murmured huskily.

"Well, she's not ready. Okay? Back off." Amy tried to move away but Mark gently caught her shoulders. His touch was sending waves of longing crashing through her. Part of her desperately wanted to give in, to fall into his arms and let him teach her to feel again, but she couldn't. She just couldn't.

"What's it going to take to make her risk it?" asked Mark, his voice like soft velvet.

"Someone a whole lot safer than you!" she said, with a catch in her voice. She pushed his hand off her shoulder and shoved past him. "Please don't. I can't do this." She dumped the bottle and glasses on the porch table and hurried towards the stairs.

"Amy, Wait!" Mark called after her, but she bolted up the stairs without turning back.

Chapter Sixteen

Amy shut the door to her room, leaned back against it trembling, and slid slowly down to the floor. She closed her eyes and exhaled slowly, trying to calm her racing heart. This was not how she'd imagined falling in love again. Fear and anxiety warring with desire and longing.

She'd imagined someone safe and secure. Someone steady and responsible. Someone who wouldn't be a risk to hurt her again. She'd never imagined falling for someone like Mark with his mysterious past. There were just too many risks involved to ever allow herself those kinds of feelings for him.

Yet, here she was. She couldn't fool herself any longer. Mark, with his dark good looks and deep blue eyes, was slowly and systematically chipping through her defenses. He was kind to her. He laughed at her jokes. He made dinner for her. Most unbelievably, he listened to her, really listened, and noticed when she was upset. Amy sucked in a long ragged breath.

It might almost be worth the risk to let down her walls just a bit, but how could she? There was a whole other side to him. He had a past he couldn't remember. If he really was as great as he seemed, then why was someone trying to kill him? If he was so perfect, wouldn't some other woman have claimed him long ago? There were so many things going on that she couldn't possibly understand.

Amy brushed the hair off her face roughly. She was just being stupid! Stupid! What would happen when his memory finally returned? He'd go back to his old life of course. A life without her. Surely he'd have people he loved, a job, commitments. He'd have to go back even if he did like her. He must realize that himself. What did he want from her then? Was she just some dalliance to pass the time because he was bored?

"I will not be someone's temporary plaything!" she hissed to herself. "Never again."

Amy slowly climbed to her feet and crossed the room to the little writing desk positioned in front of her bedroom window. She pulled up a chair, sat down, and gazed out at the view. The last few rays of the setting sun highlighted the treetops in the valley below and glinted off the lake. She could see Mark below her, too, leaning against the porch railing, looking at the same scene as she.

His back was turned towards her and he hunched forward with his left leg bent, favoring it. As she watched, he heaved a big sigh, straightened up and turned back towards the house. He slowly made his way back inside, limping heavily.

Amy tried to swallow the lump in her throat. He seemed so alone down there. It must be unnerving to know someone's trying to kill you and not be able to remember who or why. Amy closed her eyes, imagining how she'd feel if she were he. She could see herself constantly looking over her shoulder, jumping at every noise, and trusting no one. She could feel the frustration of not being able to remember, and the increasing desperation to recall something, anything. Even pretending caused an uncomfortable feeling in the pit of her stomach.

Amy sat back with a sigh and stretched to try to dispel the tightness in her chest. So maybe he wasn't just trying to use her. Maybe he was just seeking comfort from the only companion he had. If only she could get her wayward heart under control, she could be the friend he needed without risking a broken heart.

Reaching into her desk, she pulled out a well-worn Bible. Her first line of defense when life became complicated. She needed to read, pray. Reverently, she opened the book, smoothed its delicate pages, and let God speak to her heart. Somehow she always found a passage that met her current need.

As she read, God showed her: *"Trust in the Lord with all your strength, and lean not on your own understanding. In all your ways acknowledge Him and He will make your path straight."*

Several hours later, Amy felt enough at peace to put her Bible away. She got up and stretched, yawning. It was late but she felt like having a drink of juice so she made her way quietly downstairs.

The TV was talking quietly to itself when she entered the living room. Looking around, she could see Mark had cleaned everything up from their meal.

That must have been hard on his leg. Guilt washed over her. She should have helped instead of running off like a coward.

Mark was lying on the couch where he'd fallen asleep watching a show. Bella snoozed on the floor beside him, as was her new custom. Amy went over, took the throw blanket off the back of the couch, and draped it over him. After getting a glass of orange juice, she came back and sat across from him.

She leaned back, sipping her juice, and studying his face. The bruising was almost completely gone, but he still looked exhausted. Amy frowned, puzzled. His leg was healing well. He was eating well, too. She was sure his energy levels should have improved by now, but he always seemed so tired. She'd given him the very comfortable guest bed, yet most of the time he was either awake before she was, or she found him sleeping on this uncomfortable old couch. Amy shook her head slowly. Men were incomprehensible.

She was about to go back upstairs when Mark frowned and made a small noise in his sleep. His eyes rolled behind closed lids. Amy smiled to herself. He was dreaming. She sat back to watch over him a moment longer. His hand twitched reflexively. He flinched and turned his head as his breathing came faster.

Amy leaned forward a bit, frowning. Mark moaned softly as his arm flexed slightly. His whole body tensed. This was looking more like a nightmare than a dream. She hesitated, unsure if she should wake him or not. Mark's breathing was coming harder, more ragged, and sweat dotted his forehead. He flinched again. Amy was about to reach out to wake him when he suddenly bolted upright with a hoarse cry and sat, staring at nothing, gasping for breath and shaking.

"Mark?" Amy said softly, causing him to jump and whip his head in her direction. He closed his eyes in relief when he saw it was her, and leaned back against the couch, still shaking, as she continued, "Are you okay?"

"Yeah. Fine," he whispered, looking the other way.

She moved to sit beside him on the couch. "That was a pretty wicked nightmare from the looks of it."

"I guess," he replied, still avoiding her eyes. He leaned forward, putting his head in his hands, still breathing heavily.

He stiffened momentarily as Amy slipped her arm across his back, and then he slowly relaxed a bit as she began to gently rub his back up and down, like a mother might do for a child. Gradually, the tension eased from his shoulders and the tremors running through him lessened.

"I'm going to get you some juice. It'll make you feel better." Amy got up before Mark could reply and returned with a large glass of orange juice. "Drink this," she urged gently sitting beside him again.

Mark accepted the glass and began drinking slowly, still avoiding eye contact.

"Does this happen often?" she asked, a suspicion beginning to form in her mind.

Mark shrugged noncommittally.

Amy's eyes narrowed. "Is this the reason you're always down here on the couch instead of in a comfortable bed upstairs? Is this why you always look so tired? You're having these nightmares a lot, aren't you?"

Mark shrugged again, his face neutral as he continued to look off across the room. Amy gently reached up and turned his face towards her. He didn't resist but didn't meet her eyes either.

"You want me to open up to you?" she asked softly.

He finally looked at her, his face still a blank mask.

"You first," she prodded.

She watched him study her face. Bella still snoozed at their feet, unperturbed. As if finally making a decision, Mark broke off eye contact, sighed and leaned back against the couch again. He ran one hand through his already tousled hair.

"Yeah. I get nightmares. A lot."

"Why didn't you say anything?"

He shrugged again. "Dunno. It's kind of embarrassing I guess." Franz jumped up on the couch from wherever he'd been hiding and sauntered over to curl up on Mark's lap. He started stroking the cat's soft, orange fur automatically.

"Embarrassing?"

"Yeah," he said softly, focusing all his attention on the cat in his lap. "You know. Waking up, screaming and shaking like a little kid. Not very macho."

Amy smiled reassuringly. "I wouldn't exactly call it screaming."

"No?"

"No. More like a yell maybe. What are your dreams about? Can you remember?"

Mark looked away again, clearly uncomfortable. "Yeah." He hesitated. "I remember parts of them, anyway. I'm not sure, but... um... they may be memories from my past."

"Oh," Amy said, dismayed. She sat back a bit, unsure what to say next. It couldn't be good if your memories were the stuff of nightmares.

"I keep dreaming about this one couple. I feel like I should know them, but I can't remember who they are." Mark swallowed past the lump in his throat. "They, um... they always wind up dead."

Mark opened his mouth as if to say more, then stopped and focussed on the cat again.

"What?" Amy prompted.

"Nothing."

"You were going to say something. Come on. Give,"

Mark looked up at the ceiling. "It's just, maybe Dale's right. Maybe I can't remember because, subconsciously, I don't want to remember."

Amy slipped her hand into Mark's. "They're just dreams, Mark. Dreams are always worse than reality. Maybe your subconscious is just trying to sort your memories out and is getting them all confused."

"Maybe. I hope so." He looked her directly in the eye then, his own expression somewhat haunted. "If you could see what's in my dreams, Amy. If that's what my life is like, I don't think I want to remember."

"Even if those nightmares are real memories, just because you remember doesn't mean you have to go back to that life if you don't want to. You can always choose something different for yourself."

Mark half laughed. "Just that easy? Just choose differently?"

"Yes. That easy. I heard of one fellow. He was a successful lawyer or something. Anyway, one day he decided he wasn't happy with his life so he quit his job, sold his house and almost all his possessions, packed one small bag and went traveling around the world. Just like that."

"Well, that's something to think about, I guess." He regarded her with sleepy eyes, still holding her hand, caressing it with his thumb.

"You know," Amy said tentatively, "maybe if you asked God, He'd help you remember."

Mark snorted. "Oh come on, Amy! I've done everything I can think of to remember. Saying some stupid prayer isn't going to make any difference at all."

"Don't knock it 'til you've tried it. What have you got to lose?"

Mark shook his head at her in disbelief, then yawned widely. Blinking owlishly, he said, "Thanks for making me talk. It helped. I may even try to sleep upstairs tonight."

"Good." She smiled, giving his hand a little squeeze before letting go. "I'll get your crutches. Tomorrow we should probably remove those staples in your leg. It's been long enough."

She paused outside his room as he went in. "Good night, Mark," she said softly.

He smiled in response. "Good night, Amy. Sleep well."

Amy returned to her own room feeling pleased with herself. She'd been right. All he needed was a little human comfort. She'd held his hand and rubbed his back a bit. He felt better, she felt better, and no one got their feelings hurt. If she could just keep it up, everything would work out fine.

She resolutely stomped on the little voice in the back of her mind that kept whining about wanting a whole lot more from Mark than just comfort. Silly little voice. Shut up!

Chapter Seventeen

Candace carefully wrapped the still form of the little white poodle in a soft blanket, cradling him gently. Amy stood with her arm around Mrs. Dawson's frail shoulders as they shook with quiet sobs.

"I am so sorry," Amy consoled softly, tears pricking the back of her own eyes. "You've done the kindest thing for him. He's been such a good little dog for so many years. It would have been cruel to let him suffer any further. "

"I know, dear," Mrs. Dawson whispered tearfully. "But I shall miss him so. Whatever shall I do without him?"

Amy just patted her shoulder tenderly. It was far too soon to suggest a new dog to replace the old. "I hate to have to ask this, but would you prefer us to have him cremated or would you rather take him home to bury him?"

"Oh, dear. I do wish I could have him buried in my yard, but I couldn't possibly dig a hole myself. I guess I'll have to have him cremated. It's all I can do." A fresh wave of tears coursed down her wrinkled cheeks.

Amy thought for a moment. "If you want, I could come over tomorrow and bury him for you."

Mrs. Dawson looked up at Amy through teary eyes and, in a wavering voice, said, "You would? Oh, that would be lovely, dear. I would like that so much. Thank you."

"I'll be there tomorrow, about four o'clock."

By the time Amy had tidied everything up half an hour later, she still had an ache in her heart over Mrs. Dawson's loss. She offered Mark only a watery smile in response to his greeting when she entered the house. Without talking, she wandered out onto the deck and stood against the rail, shoulders hunched, looking out over the valley. Mark joined her a few minutes later.

"What's wrong?" he asked softly. "Are you okay?"

Amy smiled ruefully to herself. It amazed her how Mark always noticed her mood, whether happy or sad, no matter how subtle the signs. David had never noticed if she was upset, or, if he did, he'd never cared enough to comment.

"I had to put Mrs. Dawson's little poodle to sleep this afternoon.'" Amy brushed a tear from her cheek. "You'd think I'd be used to doing things like that by now, but it's still the toughest part of my job."

"Was he very old?"

"Ancient. She's had him for eighteen years."

"Wow," Mark murmured. "Sounds like he had a good long life though. It couldn't have been unexpected that this was coming."

"No. We've known for a while. It's tragic nonetheless. She got Barney two months before her husband died suddenly from a stroke. That little dog was her only consolation and company through that whole terrible time and he's been her only companion since. He's been her whole world for years. She'll be lost without him."

"I see. Could she get another dog?"

"That may not be practical. She's almost eighty years old herself. Her health is good at the moment, but most dogs live at least ten years or more and she may not have another ten years to give. Knowing her, she would be afraid of dying and leaving her pet with no one to care for it."

Mark remained silent for so long Amy finally glanced up at him. He stood beside her leaning with his arms crossed on the railing in front of him. He was staring out across the valley, apparently lost in thought. A breeze ruffled his hair slightly.

She longed to be able to reach up and run her fingers through his dark locks as she had when he'd first arrived. That would be far too intimate a gesture at this point. She was trying to keep things casual. Amy restrained herself, wishing for the hundredth time he could tell her something about his past. Maybe then she could allow herself to feel some of the emotions clamoring for recognition in the depths of her heart.

Mark looked down at her, finally noticing her scrutiny. He smiled a slow, wide smile that lit up his eyes and sent Amy's heart careening wildly in her chest. She quickly looked away. A cool breeze whipped her hair across her face as she shivered noticeably from her body's purely carnal reaction to his nearness.

"You're cold," Mark said as he moved to stand behind her. "Here, let me block the wind for you." He wrapped his big arms around her, pressing her back gently against his chest as he turned them slightly so his back was to the wind.

Amy relaxed back against the warm firmness of his body letting his heat penetrate her. She hadn't realized how chilled she was getting. His arms were like steel bands enfolding her. She shifted slightly and he immediately loosened his hold. Reassured that he wasn't trying to restrain her, she settled back again, closing her eyes and resting her head in the hollow between his pectoral muscles, his arms still secure around her.

They stood that way for long moments, Amy basking in the warmth of Mark's embrace. She was playing a dangerous game, she knew, but she just couldn't seem to stop herself. In his arms she felt so warm, so protected, so safe.

"Safe?" the nasty little voice in her head whispered. "Safe? He's not safe! You don't even know who he is.

Someone is trying to kill him. How safe can that be? No. This is all an illusion and you are a fool. *A fool*."

A small sob escaped her lips and tears brimmed in her eyes at the defeating words echoing in her mind.

"Amy?" Mark turned her within the circle of his arms until she was facing him. He cupped her face gently, tipping her chin up to face him. She looked up at him through spiky wet lashes.

"Sweetheart," he said, his voice caressing. "Don't cry. It'll be okay."

She dropped her lashes as a single tear trickled down her cheek. He wiped it gently away with his thumb leaving a trail of fire across her skin as he did so. Amy's heart pounded within her chest and her breath seemed to catch there. She'd never felt this way before, terrified, yet burning with desire at the same time. She looked back up, deep into his eyes. The passion reflected there mirrored what was swelling in her own heart.

He held her gaze as she waited, trapped within the spell of the moment. She couldn't look away. His head bent towards her. He hesitated, searching her face. Finally, he dropped his head farther as his lips claimed hers.

His mouth was warm and firm on her lips. His tongue teased as it caressed. The heady scent of his cologne, mingled with the salty sweet taste of him, flooded her senses and drowned her will. Amy's hands slid up the front of his chest and she began kissing him back in spite of herself.

Mark's one hand slid up to cup the back of her head, his fingers entwined in her thick mane of hair. His other hand slid down to the small of her back where it pressed her into him, sending waves of heat and longing pulsing through her body. He groaned softly as she melted into him, their kiss deepening. She felt his body respond through the thin fabric of her scrub uniform.

Alarm bells began sounding off in her mind and suddenly, unbidden, David's face was there, laughing. He was laughing at her. Laughing as he turned his back and walked away. Laughing.

Amy pushed hard against Mark's chest as she tore herself out of his embrace. "Stop!" she gasped, backing away from him with one hand outstretched as if to ward him off.

"What?..." Confusion warred with desire on his face.

"I can't... I can't do this," she sobbed, still backing away. "I don't even know who you are, what you are."

"But..."

"I'm sorry. You can't do this if you want to stay here." Amy turned and bolted off the porch.

"It wasn't just me!" Mark called out defensively, as she disappeared up the stairs.

* * *

Mark snatched the cork from Thursday night's bottle of wine off the table and threw it as hard as he could out across the yard. It floated softly to the ground. That wasn't nearly satisfying enough, but there was nothing else available to throw.

He stood with his hands on his hips, breathing hard, and letting the night breeze cool him off. He shifted a bit, trying to ease the ache in his loins. Good luck with that!

What just happened here? Mark ran one hand through his hair leaving it standing up wildly. One minute he'd experienced the most exquisite kiss, and the next....

He was sure she'd wanted him to. She'd just stood there, looking at him with those huge green eyes of hers. He'd even waited, given her a chance to pull back if he was reading her wrong. She hadn't. Instead, she'd kissed him back! He was sure of it. Then, boom! She'd pushed him away like he was trying to rape her or something. It was just a kiss!

"Arrrrgh!" Mark yelled his frustration into the night. He wanted to jump in his car and drive. Drive anywhere, as fast as he could. Drive forever. Drive until the ball of tension threatening to explode within him could dissipate. But he couldn't.

A sudden urge to go for a run flooded over him. He wanted to run and run until the sweat poured off of him, until the euphoria hit, the 'runner's high'. But he couldn't run either. The staples had come out a few days earlier and walking was still painful. He was trapped here with that amazing, tantalizing woman driving him crazy.

Mark became aware that he was pacing up and down the deck like a caged lion. His leg hurt like blazes, but the pain was a distraction from the other, more complicated feelings he was experiencing.

He considered confronting Amy and demanding some sort of explanation, but finally rejected that idea. She'd looked as confused and upset as he felt. She'd need time to cool off just as he did. Better to leave it alone for now. God knew, neither of them could go anywhere. There'd be time to talk later.

Mark continued to pace until the night breeze and gentle sounds of the nocturnal forest combined to soothe him to the point that the house didn't feel like a prison.

If he had turned and looked up, he'd have seen Amy through her bedroom window watching him, unobserved. Sadness and longing mingled with the tears on her cheeks.

Chapter Eighteen

Mark was wrong about them both being trapped. He might be, but apparently Amy was not.

She took Candace out for lunch the next day, then, after work, she informed Mark that she was going to bury Mrs. Dawson's dog. For some inexplicable reason, that took her six hours and it was well after ten before she came home. She offered him only the briefest hello as she scurried past and went up to her room.

After several more days of similar behavior it became painfully obvious that she was avoiding him at all cost. Mark did his best to be patient and keep himself amused but that was becoming increasingly difficult. There was only so much TV a fellow could watch without losing his mind completely. All of his internet searches had proved fruitless. He was still doing the cooking, but ended up eating alone. He'd even read all the interesting books she owned and had recently resorted to perusing one of the religious ones, a book called *More Than A Carpenter*.

He'd started reading it out of desperation and because it wasn't too thick. He thought he might get a laugh out of it but, surprisingly, he'd found himself more and more intrigued as the author laid out all the evidence supporting the reality of the life of Jesus Christ.

Mark had intended to read another chapter that afternoon but couldn't seem to get comfortable. He shifted positions, stretched, shifted again, and rubbed his leg. The leg was really irritating him and he couldn't tell if it was hurting or itching. He crawled off the couch and wandered over to gaze out the window.

It was a beautiful autumn day with a crystal blue sky and the barest trace of wispy white clouds. A gentle breeze ruffled through the trees and carried the scent of dry leaves and damp earth. Bella ran back and forth in the yard, barking at an unruly squirrel as it taunted her from the safety of a tree.

The urge to go jogging was getting stronger but Mark knew his leg still wasn't ready for that. Besides, he was supposed to stay hidden. This house was turning into as much of a prison as Dale's jail cell would have been. The only thing that made it tolerable was Amy's presence and now that had been removed. Mark grimaced and turned away from the window.

He needed something to do, anything to distract himself. The half-open door to the laundry room beckoned to him.

Mark hobbled upstairs to collect his laundry then limped back down again with his arms full. Pushing the door open with his shoulder, he dropped his stuff on the floor and searched the shelves for some soap. Stuffing his clothes haphazardly into the washer, he added soap and turned the machine on.

He leaned back against the wall as the washer churned and sloshed. That hadn't taken nearly long enough. Mark surveyed the little room. Unlike himself, Amy seemed to have sorted all her things into little baskets. One contained whitish stuff, another dark colors, the third was a hodgepodge of multicolored items. Mark glanced back at the washer where everything he owned, except the pajama bottoms he was wearing, currently swished around together in one big mess. Oh well, he mentally shrugged. It was all mostly dark colors anyway.

He was about to leave when he noticed one of her things had missed the basket and fallen to the floor behind it. He snatched it up, intending to toss it into the appropriate container, then hesitated as the feel of the fabric caught his attention. Mark shook out the softest, silkiest thing he had ever felt, and held it up by the shoulders. Before him was a creamy white, almost see-through satin nightie with lace trim.

Mark ogled the silky creation in his hands as his pulse began to race. In his mind's eye he could see Amy wearing this, the thin fabric cascading off the tips of her breasts and gracefully skimming the curves of her hips. She walked towards him, smiling, her arms opening to embrace him. Mark closed his eyes and leaned back against the wall with a soft groan as a wave of desire burned through him. A hint of her perfume drifted up from the fabric still clutched in his hands.

Exerting all his will, Mark forced himself to drop the nightie into the basket and leave the room. So much for getting his mind off of Amy. He ached for her with every fiber of his being.

Mark went out onto the porch and stood, leaning with his hands braced on the railing, allowing the autumn wind to slice over his bare chest. The image his mind had conjured up seemed permanently etched into his brain. It was ironic, since he'd never actually seen her wearing that nightie or anything even vaguely similar. He'd only ever seen her fully clothed or wearing thick flannel pajamas done up to the top button. It hadn't even occurred to him that she owned something so provocative.

Apparently she was trying her best not to entice him. He laughed to himself at that, because it sure wasn't working. Even dressed in a potato sack she would be irresistible.

A fresh image popped into his brain: Amy, dressed in a coarsely woven brown sack, her arms poking through the top, hands on hips, and her firm little behind barely covered by the frayed material. Mark shifted uncomfortably as another wave of desire coursed through him.

He needed some way of burning off this pent-up energy. For the millionth time he rejected the impulse to go running. Instead he went back inside, cleared a spot in the middle of the room, flicked the radio on to some fast music, and began doing sit-ups. He did them full up, then crunches, then diagonally until his abdominal muscles burned. When he couldn't force himself to do even one more he rolled over and, with his injured leg crossed over the back of the strong one, began doing push-ups. Nearly a hundred later he collapsed to the floor and lay panting for a moment. It wasn't yet enough.

Mark rolled over and sat up, scanning the room. He carefully got up and limped to the large hall closet. He opened the door, shoved all the coats to one side and examined the bar they hung on. Amy's was an old house and sturdily built, but would the bar support his weight? He tested it gingerly. It was rock solid. Good, but he couldn't hear the radio from in the closet.

Mark went back out to the radio. He hesitated only briefly before a rush of defiance washed through him and he cranked the volume up. He limped back to the closet and began doing chin-ups.

* * *

On the other side of the wall, in the clinic, Candace and Amy both looked up abruptly as the stereo suddenly blared. They both looked horrified, but for different reasons.

"What the heck is that?" Candace exclaimed, wide-eyed. "Amy, is someone in your house?"

"What? No! No, of course not. It's, um.... it's probably just the cat. He, uh, sometimes he walks on top of the stereo and bumps the 'on' button. I'll, ah, just go turn it off and check things out, okay? You just stay here with our client."

"I should come with you, just to be safe," Candace insisted.

"No, no, I'll be fine. I'm sure it's just the cat. *Please*, wait here, I'll be right back."

Amy hurried to the back of the clinic and through the door to her home, closing it firmly behind her before Candace could follow. She quickly flipped off the radio and scanned the room for Mark. Hearing something coming from the open closet door, she stormed across the room, but came to an abrupt halt when she saw Mark inside.

He was doing pull-ups, touching the back of his neck to the bar. Amy watched in wide-eyed fascination as every muscle, tendon, and sinew popped out with the effort he was exerting. A fine sheen of sweat coated his body, reflecting the light as it skimmed across his arms and chest. She felt her own temperature rise as she stood, transfixed, watching his muscles flex and relax with each repetition. Finally he dropped lightly to the floor, scooped up a towel, and rubbed the sweat from his face and chest.

"Why'd you turn off the music?" he asked belligerently. "I was listening to that."

A flare of anger brought Amy back to her senses. "Yeah? Well, so was everyone else in the clinic!" she hissed. "What were you thinking? You're supposed to stay hidden!"

"Right. Hidden. Not solitary confinement."

Amy felt a twinge of guilt as he brushed past her on his way to the couch. He plopped down, still breathing hard, as she followed him.

"Candace almost followed me in here. What if she'd seen you?"

"Good. Then maybe I'd have someone to talk to."

"But if word got out that you're here, your life could be in danger again!" Amy continued with quiet urgency.

"What do you care?" Mark snapped.

"I do care. It's just...it's complicated." Amy pleaded as Mark looked unconvinced. "Can we talk about this after work? Please?"

"Are you actually going to *be* here after work?" Mark asked skeptically.

"Yes. I promise."

Mark regarded her for long moments before saying in a softer tone, "Go back to work. I'll be quiet. For now."

Several hours later, Amy had checked and rechecked all of the animals in her care, then fed and walked Bella. Unable to find any more excuses to stall further, she took a deep breath and went through the door to her living room. Mark, fully dressed by now in track pants and a T-shirt, sat watching the news and eating a bowl of pasta. He glanced up as she came in.

"I was beginning to think you weren't going to show. There's more pasta and salad in the kitchen." He turned his attention back towards the TV.

Amy went solemnly into the kitchen and put a small amount of food on her plate. It smelled good but her stomach was in such a knot she doubted she'd be able to eat any of it. She'd agreed to talk about things later just to get him to co-operate, but she'd rather be doing just about anything else. Even going to the dentist would be preferable at the moment. Feeling slightly nauseous, she went back to the living room and sat in the armchair as far away from Mark as she reasonably could.

Mark finished his meal and waited until the news was over before turning his attention towards Amy. All she'd done in that time was push her food around in circles.

"Food no good?" he asked quietly.

"No, I'm sure it's fine. I'm just not very hungry right now." She put her plate to one side then tucked her feet up and wrapped her arms around her knees.

Had her defensive posture escaped Mark's notice? She doubted it. He sighed heavily, then got up and moved over on the couch to close the distance between them. He leaned forward with his elbows on his knees but she kept her eyes downcast.

"Look, Amy, I'm sorry I kissed you the other night. I honestly thought you wanted me to. I waited for you to pull back, and when you didn't... But I would never force you to do something you didn't want to do. Please stop running scared. I would never hurt you."

Amy looked up at him, feeling guilty. Is that what he thought she was afraid of? "No, Mark. I never thought you were trying to force me. Never."

"I see," he said, looking down at his hands. "So you, uh, just don't want me to touch you? You don't like me that way?"

The slight note of hurt in his voice tore at Amy's heart. "No, that's not it either. I do like you." She looked up and met his eyes. They were deep blue and fathomless as he searched her face for answers.

"I don't understand. If you're not afraid of me, and you like me, why are you avoiding me?"

Amy looked away again. "Because maybe I like you too much. Things could go too far."

"Too far?" Mark sounded genuinely confused. "What's that supposed to mean? If we're both attracted to each other, why not let things progress naturally?"

Amy breathed a half, humorless laugh. Now he sounded just like David had. She met his eyes. "That's just the point. It's not natural, all these people running around, doing whatever with whomever like common animals. I don't want to be your latest conquest, Mark. I want more for my life than a series of cheap, meaningless flings. The next time I sleep with a man, he's going to be my husband first."

Mark stared at her in disbelief. "Seriously?"

"Seriously. When He created it, God intended sex to be a beautiful union between two people, not a whole string of people. I want to live my life that way."

"God? Again with God? You really believe in God enough to conform your whole life to what you think He wants?"

"Yes," she said simply.

Mark sat back looking exasperated. "How do you even know there is a God out there?"

"Of course there's a God. I see His hand every day in the brilliance of a sunset or the intricacies of life. If you could just see the perfection of how bodies are designed and how all the parts interlock and work together in harmony. That's the work of a master craftsman not some random fluke of evolutionary accident. Besides, I've felt God at work in my own life ever since I asked Him to come in and forgive me. I know Jesus is real, because He's my best friend."

"Your best friend? Some mythical dead guy is your best friend?" Mark said incredulously.

"He's not mythical. There is tons of evidence to support the reality of His life. He's also not dead. Over five hundred people saw Him alive after His burial and resurrection. Plus there's the reality of my own experience. He's very, very real, Mark"

* * *

Mark frowned slightly as he watched her expression. He recalled the book he had been reading. The author had laid out so much evidence it was almost overwhelming, yet there was something within him that just didn't want to believe it.

"So why is there so much evil in the world if there's a God out there who cares? People do horrible things to each other," Mark persisted.

"Evil exists because most people don't want God to be part of their lives. They deliberately run away from Him because they don't want Him to interfere. So He stands back and gives them what they want, life without Him. What they don't understand is that, without God's protective presence, evil can easily take over. People are living wounded, broken lives and have no idea how much better life could be with God."

"But bad things still happen to good people. You aren't immune to trouble just because you believe in God," Mark countered.

"I know. The difference is, when you have God in your life, you don't go through the bad alone. He is there with you, helping you through it in a way no human friend could ever duplicate. You are never alone and never without help, or hope."

Mark studied her for a moment. She seemed so sure of what she was saying and, while she spoke, a definite peacefulness seemed to envelope her. She was pale and wary still, but there was a calm assurance that covered over the underlying anxiety. He'd never seen her look as hauntingly beautiful as at this moment.

He was loath to break the spell, but something within him still wanted to fight against all this 'God' nonsense. Besides, he wanted to learn more about her past and maybe she was in the right mood to keep talking. Cautiously he ventured, "What about your car accident? Where was God there?"

Amy looked up at him sharply, seeming shocked. "How..?"

"I looked up your name on the internet. It was all there: your skating career, the accident," Mark added softly into the stunned silence between them.

Amy sat staring down at the floor for a long time as if she was struggling to speak. "I've never talked about the accident much. Not at all really." She hugged her knees even tighter. "Everyone who knew me, all my friends and family, already knew the story so why bother talking about it? It just dredged up painful memories and regrets."

Mark fought down the urge to pull her into his arms as she spoke. This moment was so fragile. The wrong move on his part could shut down the conversation instantly. He forced himself to wait quietly, as she continued.

"So where was God? Right where He always was. It was me who had moved. I always loved Jesus, but for a while there, I wasn't really living for Him. I loved skating so much." Her voice cracked and she paused to clear it.

"I loved skating so much I guess it became an idol of sorts. All my time, energy and money went into skating. It was my whole world. There was no room for anything else, not even God."

"Then the accident happened. Everything was gone in an instant. Everything except God. Then I had a choice to make. I could blame God for everything and flounder through the loss and pain alone, or I could embrace God and allow Him to carry me through to the other side.

"I chose to embrace Him. Jesus became the rock I clung to in the storm. He kept me sane and healed most of my wounds. I still struggle with some things, but no matter what, I know God will see me through." She peeked up at him from under her eyelashes.

"If I hadn't read about the accident, I'd never have guessed you were injured," Mark ventured cautiously. "You seem perfectly fine."

Amy smiled. "God is merciful. I've healed pretty well, all things considered, but there are scars you haven't seen yet. I limp sometimes when the weather changes."

"But you never went back to skating? Not even for fun?"

"I tried it once or twice but my strength was gone. I'd broken my pelvis in two places, and my leg in three. I spent months in traction and then came the physiotherapy. When I tried to skate, I was like a beginner all over again." She sounded so forlorn, blinking back her tears. Her words broke his heart.

"I couldn't stand it, fumbling around when I used to fly. I felt like a bird with its wings clipped. I needed to move on, find a new purpose in life. That's when I decided to become a vet. I'd always loved animals," she said with a little smile, "and my time in the hospital had given me a new appreciation of medicine. I finished off my undergraduate work and transferred to the veterinary college. Now, here I am."

"Yes, here we are," Mark echoed gently. "But I can't help feeling there's more to this story you haven't shared yet."

"Well, that's all you're going to get for now," she said as the shutters closed on her expression. "It's more than I've shared with anyone else."

Mark regarded her thoughtfully for a few minutes. He debated encouraging her to reveal more but decided against it. Dale was right about her being skittish. He'd persuaded her to open up to him a bit, but if he pushed too hard he'd lose all he'd gained and then some.

Forcing himself to be patient, Mark asked, "So, what do we do about our problem? Your home is lovely Amy but it's beginning to feel like a prison to me. I must not be used to being cooped up in one place because I'm starting to go stir-crazy here. The only thing that makes it tolerable is being able to talk to you."

"I'm sorry about the past few days," Amy replied in a soft, determined voice. "I should have come and talked to you like an adult instead of hiding, but I just didn't know what to say. I like you, Mark, but there are way too many questions about your past for me to let you be anything other than just a friend. You have to promise to treat me as a friend only, and nothing more, or I'll have to call Dale and have him find you somewhere else to hide."

Mark hesitated. He wanted so much more than mere friendship, but if he pushed he'd scare her off and wind up cooling his heels in one of Dale's jail cells. The thought of that was even less appealing than having to hide his feelings from her. Mark forced a smile. "Sure, no problem. Just friends. I promise."

"Good." Amy's smile didn't quite reach her eyes. "Tomorrow's Saturday. Maybe we can sneak you out for a drive up to the accident site. You might remember something."

"Sure. It'll be nice to get out for a bit." Mark kept his voice light.

"Okay, well, I guess I'll see you tomorrow then. Good night." Amy uncurled from her spot in the chair and made her way up the stairs.

* * *

Good. He'd agreed to her demands right away. He hadn't argued or tried to persuade her to pursue a physical relationship. He hadn't even looked disappointed. Things had worked out exactly as she'd wanted.

So why did her heart feel so heavy in her chest?

Chapter Nineteen

Amy came walking towards him out of the mist. Mark stood there, waiting, rooted to the spot as she approached slowly, her hips swaying seductively under the clingy silken fabric of her white negligee. Her soft golden hair fell in loose cascades around her shoulders, framing a heart-shaped face and iridescent green eyes. Mark's eyes clung to her as she came steadily closer. His body flushed with heat, every nerve on fire with desire, yearning to touch her, unable to move. She smiled, ever so slightly, and his breath caught in his throat as their eyes met.

Then she stood before him, mere inches away, so close he could feel the heat radiating from her. Her breath fanned soft and sweet across his face. She reached out slowly, her slender, pale fingers barely touching the skin of his abdomen, and gently ran her fingers up across his chest, ruffling the hairs and causing them to stand up. He shivered as jolts of pleasure shot though him.

Finally able to move, he reached for her with a soft groan and pulled her hard against his body, his desire painful in its intensity. Her lips parted in a soft sigh as his mouth descended on hers. She surrendered completely to his kiss, her hands leaving trails of fire as they caressed his back, his chest, his hips. Mark's heart pounded as his need swelled, burning within him, driving him on. He moved his hands to her hips and slowly edged her nightie up. She smiled up at him, her lips soft and moist, her eyes hooded with desire.

Then, suddenly, she shoved him away with a laugh.

"You have to catch me first!" She spun away and sprinted off, laughing as she did.

Mark stood a moment, stunned, paralyzed.

No! He couldn't lose her now. He had to have her. She belonged with him!

He began to run, following her as she darted back and forth. His breath came hard and fast as he chased her. Her laughter floated back towards him as she remained just out of his reach. So close. So far. He ran harder, faster. She eluded him, twisting out of his reach. He came closer, closer. His hand reached out, his feet pounding the ground. Another inch, half an inch, almost there! He grabbed her arm and spun her around.

There was something wrong. Very wrong.

His heart hammered in his chest as he gasped for air, staring.

Her golden hair had become a mass of rich dark brown curls. Her emerald green eyes had darkened into cobalt blue. Her heart-shaped face had higher cheekbones and a squarer jawline. She was taller, graceful, beautiful, but she wasn't Amy. She smiled up at him adoringly.

"I knew you'd come back. I've missed you." She reached up to put her arms around his neck and whispered. "I love you."

Mark awoke with a gasp and sat up. Moonlight filtered in the bedroom window and highlighted the thin sheen of sweat that covered his body. He got up, adjusting his pajama bottoms as he did so, and wandered over to gaze out the window.

Who was the dark-haired woman? She reminded him of the other dark-haired woman in his dreams, but she was younger. She felt so familiar, like he should know her, but he couldn't connect her to a real memory. Maybe she was just a variant of the other woman. Maybe both were just products of his imagination.

Amy wasn't though. The memory of how she'd looked in his dream, of how she'd felt in his arms, washed over him. His body pulsed in response as a fresh wave of desire surged through him. Mark closed his eyes and pressed his hot forehead against the cold windowpane, trying vainly to relax. Staying here was torture, but there was nowhere else he'd rather be.

* * *

Mark slouched down in the passenger's seat, a ball cap pulled low over his eyes. Ostensibly, this was so he could duck down quickly if they passed a car Amy recognized, but really, it suited his mood at the moment. While it had been great to get out of the house for a bit, the trip had been a failure in other respects. That, combined with lack of sleep and images of Amy he couldn't get out of his head, had him in a foul humor.

They had left Amy's house several hours earlier and had driven up Summit Road, past the accident site and farther up into the mountain in the hopes that something would jar his memory. Mark had watched expectantly at first as they drove down one little back road after another, but nothing looked even vaguely familiar. His hopes sank further and further with each small homestead and cabin they passed. He didn't recognize anything, and couldn't think of a single reason why he might have been heading in that direction the night of the crash.

Amy had become quieter and quieter as the morning progressed, as if picking up on his black mood, so now Mark was surprised when she pulled the truck off onto the side of the road.

"Why are we stopping?" he asked.

"This is where you crashed."

"You showed me this on the way up."

"Yes, but I thought it might help to get out and walk around a bit."

Mark sighed. He didn't think anything was going to help anymore, but it probably wouldn't hurt either. He climbed slowly from the truck, stretched and looked around.

A chill wind caressed the mountainside, cutting through his sweater and whipping Amy's hair across her face. She tried to brush it back with one hand, but little tendrils kept escaping and dancing around her head. Mark watched, mesmerized at the display. Amy glanced up at him, questioningly, her eyes impossibly large in her tiny face. Their eyes held a moment until Mark forced himself to look away.

Hands stuffed in his pockets, he strolled down the road a short way, willing himself to recall the crash. He stared down the hill to where the road disappeared around a bend. This section looked pretty much the same as the rest of it. It was a two-lane road with wide gravel shoulders, a dirt cliff rising up the inside and a steep drop-off on the outside. The mountain was thickly treed with a mix of aspen, birch, spruce and pine, which lent a pungent, evergreen smell to the air. It reminded him of Amy's sundeck rather than his accident.

The whole morning had been that way. Instead of remembering his past, he had been thinking of Amy. Her mere presence sent waves of desire racing through him and yet, somehow, he had to feign indifference towards her.

He knew he needed to remember. Things couldn't go on like this indefinitely. He also knew that, once he remembered, there'd be no good excuse for him to stay on at Amy's place any longer.

Mark scowled and turned to look up the road in the direction he'd been traveling that night. He deliberately looked past Amy, trying not to see her, ignoring the ache in his chest.

Remembering had another drawback. He might not like what he remembered. He was still plagued regularly by nightmares; bloody, gruesome, violent things that jolted him awake and left him awake for hours. It was such a contrast to the warm, safe life he was living with Amy. Were his nightmares any reflection of his reality? He wasn't sure he wanted to find out.

It had been near nightfall when he crashed, Mark thought. He closed his eyes and tried to imagine the road in darkness. A picture flashed into his mind of a deer bounding out in front of him, the headlights suddenly illuminating it as if it had appeared by magic. He recalled hitting the brakes and turning the wheel abruptly. Then nothing. He tried for a few minutes to remember more, but it proved futile. Finally he opened his eyes to find Amy watching him intently.

"I think a deer jumped out in front of my car. That's why I hit the brakes and blew them out," Mark said simply as he moved to stand by the edge of the road overlooking the valley below.

"That's wonderful! Can you remember anything else?" Amy asked, moving to stand beside him.

"No. It's been over three weeks, and I still can't recall anything significant." Frustration edged his voice.

"It'll come. I'm sure of it," Amy said comfortingly, slipping her arm around his waist.

Mark stiffened at her touch. Gently but firmly he took her hand and removed it from his waist. "Maybe you shouldn't do that," he said in a quiet, firm voice. "Come on. Let's go." He limped back to the truck and climbed in without looking at her.

* * *

Stung, Amy followed silently and climbed into the driver's side. She focused intently on the road as she drove home, willing herself not to cry. This is what she wanted, she reminded herself. She'd asked him to keep his distance and he was respecting that. She should be relieved. She should be happy. She should, but she wasn't.

Chapter Twenty

Amy found the next few days very difficult. She spent time with Mark as promised, and they did the same types of things as before, yet the easy repartee was gone. Mark was pleasant enough, but he acted so reserved, as if he was holding something back, and their conversations didn't flow like they used to. Amy longed to put things back the way they were but couldn't think of how to do it without risking her heart even further.

Dale stopped by Tuesday evening. He stayed only long enough to express his frustration at his lack of progress in the case and to check up on Amy. He seemed to think that someone was deliberately hiding Mark's identity because he kept running into dead-ends on every line of investigation, and the fingerprints still hadn't come back. Privately, Amy thought it was just the wheels of bureaucracy grinding as slow as usual. The answers would come eventually.

When Amy came through the door Thursday after work, Mark seemed almost his old self as he greeted her enthusiastically. "Good, you're home. Come here. I want to show you something." He took her by the hand and led her to the computer.

"Look at this." He indicated a web page for a dog rescue association. "What do you think?"

"It's fine, I guess, but I already have a dog and I don't need..."

"No, not you. The elderly lady who had her poodle put to sleep last week. You said she was probably too old to take on the commitment of a new pup. This group specializes in finding homes for older dogs. They say it's easy to find homes for puppies and young animals but there are many older dogs put to sleep because no one wants them. Usually they're good dogs whose owners have to give them up for various reasons, some even because the owner died. This might be perfect for your client. She could rescue a dog in need and gain some company for herself without having to make a long commitment."

As he spoke Amy had been looking at the computer screen, a slow smile spreading across her face. "Have you been thinking about this since last week?" she asked as she turned to meet his grin.

"Off and on. What do you think?" he replied, seeming quite pleased with himself.

"I think it's a fantastic idea!" Amy grinned back, and, on impulse, threw her arms around his chest, hugging him fiercely.

* * *

Mark closed his eyes and allowed himself a brief moment of pleasure as he returned her embrace. She broke away, still grinning, obviously unaware of the emotional turmoil she was causing within him. He carefully composed his face and returned her smile.

"I can't believe you actually cared enough about an old lady you never even met to spend your time searching out a solution for her. This is perfect. Oh, I hope she likes the idea. I'm going to call her right now and see what she thinks. I'll be right back. I've just got to get my client list from the clinic."

Amy dashed off as Mark watched, still smiling. Of course, he didn't care as much about the old lady as he did about Amy herself, but he was content to let her believe what she wanted. It was so nice to see her genuinely happy again after the strain of the past week. He closed his eyes again and basked in the warm afterglow of her embrace a moment longer before heading to the kitchen to dish up supper.

They had just finished eating when the phone rang.

"Maybe that's Mrs. Dawson calling me back," Amy said, bouncing up to answer the phone.

"Hello," she answered brightly, and then her voice cooled abruptly as she continued, "I told you not to call me."

Mark frowned slightly, as he watched her face grow pale and tense.

"Can't it wait 'til tomorrow? No? All right. Come straight over. I'll meet you in the clinic." Amy put the phone down.

"What was that all about?" Mark asked, feeling uneasy.

"That was David. His dog is hurt. Apparently it's serious and can't wait," Amy said tersely.

"Why can't he use some other vet?" Mark asked, trying to hide the wave of jealousy that washed over him at the mention of David's name.

"There is no other vet. I'm it. So I'm pretty much obligated to see him. Besides, it's not the dog's fault its owner is a jerk."

Feeling somewhat mollified by her tone of disgust, Mark asked, "What can I do to help?"

"Just stay out of sight. You absolutely cannot let David see you. He'll tell anyone who'll listen that you're here. I'll treat the dog and get him out of here as soon as possible. It shouldn't take long." Amy got up half-heartedly. "I guess I should get in there and set up what I'll need."

It took all of Mark's willpower to just sit there and let Amy walk back into the clinic. The moment the door closed he was up and limping restlessly around the room. He had a bad feeling about this.

If David's dog really was hurt, and Amy was the only vet in town, then he would have to call her. Nothing suspicious there. Dogs don't always choose to injure themselves during office hours, so the timing wasn't necessarily suspicious either. Still, Mark couldn't shake the feeling that something wasn't quite right.

Perhaps it was that picture of Amy staring up at David with adoring eyes that Mark couldn't seem to get out of his head. She didn't seem that enamored of David now, but she had certainly been infatuated with him back then. Had there been more to it than just a crush? Was there any chance the old feelings could come back?

He needed to know and it was driving him crazy.

Mark snatched up a pencil and began fiddling with it nervously. Was he just being irrationally jealous? That was a distinct possibility, too.

He continued pacing until the sound of tires on gravel caught his attention. Mark walked into the kitchen and cautiously peered out the window towards the parking area. Bella jumped up and put her paws on the window ledge to look, too. Mark was surprised to hear a low growl come from the dog as a tall blonde man climbed out of a new SUV and headed around the corner towards the clinic door. He cursed the poor lighting which prevented him from getting a better look at David and his injured dog. Mark stood at the window, staring at where David had disappeared, mouth set in a grim line, pencil flipping and twirling in his fingers.

Chapter Twenty-One

Amy sat at the clinic front desk absently flipping the pages of a medical journal while her leg vibrated up and down rapidly. She had prepped the exam room and the surgery table, just in case, and had double-checked the supplies in the medicine locker. There was nothing else left for her to do but wait.

She had always hated waiting when she was younger. She would drive everyone else around her crazy with her impatience. Months in rehab after her accident however, had done much to develop her patience. That is, most of the time, but this business of David showing up on short notice had her rattled.

Amy startled abruptly as the door opened, almost dropping her magazine. Mentally cursing herself for being so jumpy, she took a deep breath and turned to meet David for the first time in over twelve years.

Tall and slim with thick wavy blonde hair, he still radiated confidence and charisma as he entered the room. He smiled when he saw her, his undeniable charm just as palpable as ever. Amy wasn't fooled though. She knew only too well that all this was just a cover-up for whatever was currently on his agenda.

"Amy, darling. It's great to see you again," David said in dulcet tones, his smile ever present.

"David," Amy greeted him coolly. "Where's this injured dog of yours?"

"That's my Amy. Always straight down to business. You haven't changed a bit," he said, looking towards the waiting area to his right, and moving through it to poke his head into the exam room beyond. "Nice little set-up you have here. Lots of room. Really private."

"Thank you. I like it," Amy answered curtly, starting to follow him. What was he up to? "About your dog...."

"She's in the SUV. I wanted to check out your clinic before I brought her in. What's back here?" he asked, moving past her to the surgical room.

"My surgery room and some kennels in the recovery area where we keep the sick and injured animals if they have to stay."

"Hmm, nice," he said, strolling into the room, then turning back towards her. "It's big. Do you run this all by yourself?"

"I usually have an assistant, Candace, but she's already gone home for the night."

"So we're all alone here?"

"Yes. Will that be a problem? Is your dog hard to handle?" Amy said trying to curb her impatience.

"No, no. He's a pussy cat, figuratively speaking that is." David stepped towards her, flashing an engaging smile as he moved in closer.

Amy's return smile was strained. He was the same old David, still using his charm and good looks to run the show. He always had to be in control, do things on his own timetable, steer the conversation where he wanted it to go. She used to admire that in him, thinking it revealed confidence and capability. Now she just found it annoying. Having to control everything merely showed his insecurity, rather than confidence.

Of course he was still as handsome as ever, though now that she was closer to him, Amy thought he seemed a bit too slim, and his face seemed a bit gaunt. Perhaps he had been ill. One thing was becoming more and more clear to her though. The magic was gone.

She'd been so afraid of running into him, thinking that if she saw him it would rekindle all her old feelings and reopen all the old pain. Now, in reality, seeing him face to face, she felt very little towards him. There were no butterflies, no wrench of the heart, no stab of pain, only a trace of regret that she'd wasted so many years stressing out about him. Had he not been watching her expectantly at that moment she might have laughed with relief.

Then something tweaked in her mind. The sense of wrongness solidified.

"'He'? You said, 'He's a pussycat.' But you said 'she' was in the car. Is your dog male or female? And where is your dog? You said this was an emergency that couldn't wait but you've done nothing but stall since you got here."

David's smile faltered a moment before he recovered and moving even closer said, "Ah, Amy. I never could slip anything past you, could I? You've always been so perceptive, at least most of the time. Actually, there is no dog. I just wanted a chance to talk to you, one on one. I've... missed you." He reached towards her to touch her cheek but she pulled back to stay just beyond his reach.

"So what you're saying is, that you lied to me and tricked your way in here after hours, is that right?" Amy accused, her temper starting to rise. "You're trying to manipulate me, again."

The sound of a small piece of wood snapping echoed from the far back of the room.

"Darling. Lied is such a harsh word. I prefer the word 'persuaded'. Besides, I just wanted to see you." He moved a little closer to her as she retreated a step farther back into the surgical room.

"Why? Why after all these years do you suddenly want to see me?" Why was he acting so creepy?

"It hasn't been sudden for me," he wheedled. "I've been thinking about this for a while now. Breaking things off with you was a mistake. I see that now." He continued to move slowly towards her.

"So what? Surely you're not asking for us to get back together again after all this time." She retreated still farther, her anxiety starting to build.

"Why not? We were always great together. There's no reason why we couldn't be great again."

"Except that I don't love you anymore and I'm not interested in picking up where we left off. You should leave now," Amy said firmly. She took another step back and bumped into the corner of the room.

David's lips curled in the imitation of a smile, though there was no warmth in it. "Amy, Amy, Amy. You always say no when you really mean yes." He stood uncomfortably close to her and reached up to caress her cheek with his hand. His touch made her skin crawl.

She tried to pull away, bumping her head on the wall. "Stop it! I told you to leave." She pushed his hand away from her and tried to move past him out of the corner, but he braced his hand on the wall blocking her in with his arm. His other hand slid up behind her head and grabbed a handful of hair which he used to force her head back so she had to look at him.

Amy's heart throbbed in her chest. She should never have met with him alone. She knew that now, but it was too late. She should have called Candace back in to assist her. Mark was only a room away but she couldn't call for him. His life depended on staying hidden. Somehow, she had to handle this on her own.

David pressed in even closer. His breath washed warm across her face as he waited, inches from her, seeming to enjoy watching the anger in her eyes turn to fear.

"Stop it!" she hissed, pushing hard against his chest as her pulse pounded in her ears. "Leave me alone! I already have a boyfriend."

David chuckled softly as he tightened his grip on her hair, causing her to wince. "Who's a liar now? I already checked around town. You don't have a boyfriend. You don't even date." He smiled knowingly, his other hand sliding insolently up the side of her body as he pressed her into the wall.

David bent to kiss her just as Mark's voice cut harshly through the air from behind them. "Is something wrong with your hearing, or are you just stupid? The lady told you to leave her alone!"

David dropped Amy so abruptly she would have fallen had she not already been pressed back against the wall. Relief and gratitude flooded over her as she sagged against the wall. How had he known? She didn't care. He was there and that was all that mattered. Heart in her throat, Amy watched as David spun to find Mark standing casually, near the doorway between the surgery and Amy's living room. His stance seemed relaxed, nonchalant even, but Amy could see a cold fury burning in his eyes.

She slid out from behind David and inched along the wall to her left, where she was out of reach but could see both men. Shaking, she watched David straighten and take a few steps towards Mark.

His eyes narrowed as he snarled, "Who the hell are you?"

"I'm her *boyfriend*. Now get out," Mark replied in a cold, hard voice.

"Boyfriend?" David said as a calculating look came to his face. "She doesn't have a boyfriend! Nobody's even heard of you."

"And yet, here I am," Mark drawled insolently.

"You," David emphasized, "are interfering in a *private* conversation between my fiancée and me. You get out." He moved to within a few feet of Mark and stood staring him eye to eye.

"Ex!" Amy exclaimed. "Ex-fiancée. Very ex!" She cast a fearful glance at Mark, unsure how he'd react to the bombshell David had just dropped. If it had caught him off-guard, he gave no sign. Mark remained relaxed but ready as he leaned one shoulder against the wall and a condescending smile spread across his face.

"Seems your *ex*-fiancée doesn't care to talk to you anymore. Maybe that's because the girl is mine now and is well over you. Or maybe, she'd just forgotten all about you. Come to think of it, I've been living with her for three weeks now and she's never even mentioned your name in all the time I've known her."

David's face dropped in disbelief. "Living with her? She refused to live with me. Why in hell would she live with you? She *adored* me. I was the best thing that ever happened to her! She's been pining for me for years! Everybody says so!"

"Guess you're wrong about that, aren't you? Obviously, the only person who adores you, is you," Mark goaded, the laughter on his lips not reflected in the glittering hardness of his eyes.

Anger contorted David's face as the insult sank in. Amy gasped as David pulled back his fist and threw a punch straight at Mark's face. Almost too fast to see, Mark blocked David's punch, grabbed his wrist, swung him around and slammed him into the wall with his arm twisted up behind his back. Mark leaned on him hard and wrenched the arm just a little farther until David gasped in pain.

"That," Mark whispered ominously into David's ear, "was a really stupid thing to do. If you ever try a stunt like that again, I'll break your arm right off! Now get out of here and don't come back. Ever!"

Mark released David and shoved him towards the door. David stumbled forward, then straightened and turned back towards Mark. Absently rubbing his shoulder, he bathed Amy and Mark alternately with a look of pure hatred.

"You'll be sorry!" he hissed in their direction.

"I'm already sorry I didn't break your arm. Get going before I decide to remedy that," Mark said taking a step in his direction.

With a final glare of loathing, David spun on his heel and stormed through the waiting room and out of the clinic. His SUV showered the side of the building with gravel as he peeled out of the parking lot.

Amy still stood with her back against the wall, hand over her mouth, pulse racing. She was staring at Mark who, in turn, was staring out the office window at the cloud of dust left behind by the SUV's hasty departure. He had his hands clenched and was still breathing hard from the confrontation. Finally he turned his attention back towards Amy.

"Are you all right?" he asked, walking quickly towards her.

She nodded dumbly as he pulled her into the shelter of his arms and stood just holding her for a few minutes.

With her head nestled on his chest, she could hear his heart hammering like a drum. Apparently he hadn't felt as calm as he had looked. On some level, perhaps he really did care about her. She smiled a bit to herself, but then the magnitude of what he had just done began to sink in.

He released her as she pulled back and said, "Mark, what have you done? He saw you. Your hiding spot is blown."

"Yeah, I know. I had no choice, did I?"

"But he could tell anyone. He *will* tell everyone, maybe even the men looking for you."

"Maybe, but not likely. What are the chances your old...fiancé," he said, stumbling over the word, "knows the men who sabotaged my car?"

"But still, what if..?"

Amy swallowed down a cold ball of fear that sat in the pit of her stomach like a rock. In spite of her efforts to guard her own heart, Mark had slid past her defenses and was far more important to her than she wanted to admit. The thought of him being in danger terrified her. All she could think of was him dead or dying. "You shouldn't have come back here," she started.

"And what was I supposed to do, Amy?" he snapped. "Hide in the back room while you get raped? What kind of a coward do you think I am?"

Amy's face paled. "You're not a coward. You're the bravest man I know but…but... Oh, I'm so stupid! I should never have let him come over." Tears brimmed in her eyes. If Mark got hurt because of her...

"Hey, don't do that," Mark said, his tone softening instantly as he knelt in front of her and wiped a tear from her cheek. "You didn't know. He lied, remember?"

"Yes, but I *know* him. I should have suspected something like this. And now you're in danger again and it's all my fault," she added woefully.

Mark gave her a slightly lopsided smile. "Don't worry about it. That's what boyfriends are for, hmm?"

"Except you aren't *really* my boyfriend. I lied about that part." She confessed, eyes locked on his. Her heart ached as she saw his smile fade. "We're just friends, right?"

The thought crossed her mind that none of her previous boyfriends would ever have risked themselves like that, let alone guys who were just friends. The implication was too much to deal with. Amy shoved the thought to the back of her mind for later.

"Right. Just friends," he said quietly, standing up. "Come on. Let's go back into your place and call Dale. He should know what's happened."

Mark stood up and gave her hand a little tug to draw her after him. She allowed herself to be led back into her home, still mentally grappling with what had happened.

She absently stepped over a broken pencil lying in the doorway.

How was she ever going to thank him?

Chapter Twenty-Two

Amy mentally kicked herself for not seeing what David was up to sooner. He'd always been selfish and willing to do almost anything to get what he wanted, but he'd never been violent before. When had he changed? Perhaps it had always been there and she had just been too naive to see it. She silently shook her head.

Then there was the puzzle of Mark, himself. Someone had already gone to great lengths to try to kill him, and they were probably still out there, looking for him. He still couldn't remember anything, so he was completely vulnerable to attack. It could come from anywhere. Yet he'd opened himself up just to protect her. Why?

Amy curled up on the couch while Mark talked to Dale on the phone. He had his back to her, strong and broad in a fitted T-shirt. He'd been so masterful during that confrontation, calm, cool, and totally in charge. David usually walked all over people but it hadn't worked with Mark. She remembered again how quickly and decisively he'd slammed David into the wall. Mark hadn't shown a hint of weakness even though he was limping heavily now.

Where'd he learn a move like that? She watched him silently, totally lost in her own thoughts.

Had he only protected her because he thought he owed her for rescuing him from the car wreck? Was it just obligation, or maybe it was some innate sense of gallantry dictating that he must protect the damsel in distress? Could there be any more to it than that? Could he possibly have real feelings for her besides mere lust?

She'd thought David had loved her, but that had turned out to be just his selfish desire to possess her. That's why she'd written off Mark's overtures as simply a mixture of loneliness and natural male lust. He'd use her and move on when he was finished, just like David had done. All men were basically the same after all, weren't they? Weren't they?

She was beginning to wonder if she'd made the wrong assumptions. Even if she had, it still didn't change the fact that he could leave at any moment and never return.

"Amy? Amy!"

"Huh? Sorry, were you saying something?" She brought her attention back to Mark who had put the phone down and was now facing her.

"I was saying Dale's going to hunt down David and have a little talk with him about keeping his mouth shut or else. If he talks to anyone, Dale's going to charge him with assaulting you. Actually, I'll be surprised if he doesn't charge him anyway. Dale was really angry when he heard what happened. You will testify if it comes to that, won't you?" Mark's tone was rather more commanding than inquiring, as if daring her to say no.

"Do you really think that'll be necessary? I'm sure he's learned his lesson..."

"Necessary? Of course it's necessary! He assaulted you! It would have been worse if I hadn't been there!" Mark snapped.

Amy hesitated, taken aback by his sudden anger.

"Okay. I get it," Mark said sharply as he turned his back and crossed the room to the window. "I forgot you were engaged at some point. You still have a soft spot for him and can't bear for him to get in trouble no matter what he does."

"No, it's not like that. It's just, well, nothing really happened and..."

"And that makes it okay?"

"Of course not, but..." Amy's voice pleaded as he continued to stand rigidly facing the window.

"Look, Amy. I can probably never repay you for all you've done for me, but I think I've been here long enough. My cover's blown anyway so I might as well leave. Call Dale to come pick me up." He turned abruptly and stalked off towards the stairs.

"Wait!" Amy leapt off the couch to catch his arm.

He paused, body rigid, refusing to look at her, but waiting nonetheless. "What?"

"Why are you so angry with me? I don't understand," she pleaded.

He didn't answer at first, just stared up at the ceiling while a little muscle twitched in his jaw. Finally he turned towards her angrily and said, "I kiss you and you completely freak out. David backs you into a corner and attacks you, but 'nothing really happened'! How's that supposed to make me feel?" He pulled his arm from her grasp.

"I, I never thought of it that way..."

"Yeah? Well, it seems pretty obvious. You're still in love with him despite what you say."

"No, I'm not! Maybe I was a long time ago, but not now. You don't understand what he did."

"No, I don't. You won't tell me a thing." He turned away from her to gaze out the dark window. "You never even mentioned you'd been engaged," he added so softly she almost couldn't hear him.

"Because it's humiliating," she said quietly. "I... I'll tell you now, if you want to hear it."

"Whatever," he said derisively, but remained standing there, staring out the window, waiting for her to speak.

"Come sit down." She reached tentatively for his hand. "You're making me nervous, standing there."

She led him back to the couch where he sat and leaned back to stare pointedly at the ceiling with his arms crossed in front of him. Amy sighed. He was being so difficult. It was almost like his feelings were hurt. Why would he care so much? He was just going to leave soon anyway.

Maybe she should let Dale come get him after all. It might be better in the long run for both of them. The thought of him leaving, however, caused such an ache in her chest that she shoved the idea away and focused her mind elsewhere.

He'd stuck his neck out for her. He deserved an explanation. Then if he still wanted to leave, she'd cope somehow.

Amy sat on the couch beside Mark, hugging her knees as was her custom when talking about something difficult. She closed her eyes a moment, asking God for His wisdom, and then softly started to speak.

"We got engaged while we were skating partners. We were so young. I was sure I was in love and that he loved me, too. Of course, he wasn't a Christian so I should never have agreed to marry him, but I wasn't really living like a Christian myself so it didn't matter to me at the time. I realize now what a big mistake that was."

Mark continued staring at the ceiling, saying nothing.

"Anyway, things were fine until the accident. I remember waking up in the hospital in so much pain and wondering where he was, if he was okay. My mom was there. She told me he was fine but wouldn't say much more. I guess she was trying to protect me.

"I didn't see him for a few days, but I was heavily medicated and slept a lot. I thought I was just asleep when he came by. I was wrong."

Amy kept talking softly as she relived that one final day...

Twelve years ago...

She lay flat on her back with her leg elevated in traction. The nurses had just finished re-bandaging her hands and checking on the incisions from the surgery which had seen metal plates screwed into her pelvis to hold it together.

"I see you haven't used any pain meds in a while. Are you sure you don't want something? It's awfully soon to stop taking them," her matronly nurse asked kindly.

"No, thank you. My fiancé called to say he's coming over and I want to be awake when he gets here. I keep sleeping through his visits," Amy said weakly.

The nurse gave her an odd look. "All right, but I'll be back after his visit to give you something. No arguments."

Amy nodded her agreement then lay staring at the clock for another hour before she heard David's voice down the hall. He was laughing at something.

"David!" she called joyously as he came through the doorway. Her face fell as a pretty brunette followed him in a moment later.

"Hello, darling," he said cheerfully. "Sorry I haven't been to see you 'til now but you know how busy our training schedule is. You know Darla here from the club, right?" He indicated the brunette who smiled back at him coyly.

"You, you haven't been here 'til now? I thought I had just missed your visits."

"Yeah, sorry. Busy training. You know how it is."

"How can you be training? I'm your partner." Amy struggled to understand what was happening. The pounding in her head didn't make it any easier.

"About that. The doctors say there's no way you're going to be ready to compete in the Olympics this year. No way at all."

"What? No... No one told me..."

"Yeah, well, it's the truth. Can't do anything about it. But I still have a chance to go if I get a new partner. That's where Darla here comes in. She's agreed to step in and be my new partner! Isn't that great?" David said grinning ear to ear.

"Yeah. Great," Amy answered flatly.

Darla smiled sweetly up at David as if Amy weren't there.

"Did the doctors say when I'll be able to get out of here?" Amy asked forlornly.

"I don't remember exactly. Two months? Three? Something like that." He was looking at Darla as he spoke.

"Oh good." Relief washed over her. "I was afraid we'd have to postpone our wedding. I may not be ready to skate in the Olympics but I'll be healed enough to get married when you get back." Amy's feeling of relief faded as she watched Darla try to hide a smirk behind her hand.

"Yeah... about that… I'm afraid the wedding's off. Sorry," he added with not the slightest hint of regret in his voice.

Amy's jaw dropped. "But... but I love you. I...you.... you said you loved me, too."

"Oh come on, Amy! You didn't really think we were going to go through with it? Me? Marry you?"

Darla giggled.

"B-but I.....But we..." Amy's face flamed with embarrassment. "But we already did it. I only slept with you because you were going to marry me."

"And I only asked you to marry me because you wouldn't put out unless I did." David smirked. "If you weren't so unreasonable this would have never happened. It's all your own fault, you know."

Amy just stared at him, open-mouthed, as a terrible pain crushed down on her chest. In her world, the fairy-tale castle cracked. It started small, at the base, and spread up, branching and re-branching as the castle fractured into smaller and smaller fragments. Then the pieces started to fall, individually at first, then more and more until the whole thing cascaded down through Amy's heart like a million splinters of glass, slicing as they fell. She lay there, silent and glassy-eyed, as something died on the inside.

Darla giggled. "I can't believe she actually thought you'd marry her! Come on, let's go. This is boring."

"Gotta go, Amy. I'll see you around sometime." David barely glanced at her before turning to follow Darla.

He said something inaudible as they left causing Darla to break into peals of laughter. The last thing Amy heard was David's voice ringing down the hall, laughing and laughing, until a door slammed and it was gone.

* * *

Amy sat in silence for a long time after telling her story to Mark. When she finally came back to the present and turned to look at him, she found him no longer staring at the ceiling but watching her intently, a strange mixture of anger and something else on his face.

"I've never told anyone else the whole story before you. My friends and family know he dumped me, but not all the details."

"I should have broken his arm while I had the chance," Mark muttered savagely. "It's no wonder you hate him."

"But I don't hate him. I forgave him years ago," she said softly.

Mark scowled in response, clearly confused. "How could you? After the way he used you and left you all alone in that hospital, how could you just forgive him?"

"For one thing, I wasn't alone. God was still with me even though I hadn't been with Him." Amy sighed and leaned closer to Mark, willing him to understand. "I chose to forgive him, not because he deserved it, but for my own sake, so I could heal. I would have destroyed myself if I had nursed a grudge against him. Forgiving him was the only way to let God come in and heal all the broken pieces. And I am healed. I just never realized it 'til now.

"You see, David kind of did me a favor tonight. I've spent the last twelve years of my life avoiding him like the plague. I wouldn't go anywhere that he might be - that's the other reason I stopped skating - and everyone knew better than to as much as mention his name. I was so afraid that seeing him, or talking about him, would rip open all the old wounds and bring back all the old pain that I ran scared all the time.

"I was finally forced to face him tonight, and it wasn't nearly as bad as I thought it would be. I found out I don't have any feelings left for him at all. Nothing. That's when I knew I was finally, truly, free of him." Amy sighed in relief. "I guess that's why I'm not eager to take this to court. You stepped in before any real harm was done, and his kiss meant nothing to me."

Mark was still scowling, clearly trying to come to grips with what she was saying. Amy waited for his next question.

"So, the reason you freaked out when I kissed you is because..." Mark led off.

"Is because of how it made me feel. I - I think I might be falling for you, Mark, but let's face it, you could wake up with your memory back at any time, and walk out of my life forever," Amy finished. "I just can't risk being hurt like that again, ever."

"But I'm not David. I'm not like him at all. I would never walk out on you like that. I..."

"Don't," she said softly, touching her fingertips to his lips to silence him. "There are some things you just can't say until you know who you are. There are some promises you shouldn't make until you know you can keep them."

"Who says I can't keep them? I know what's in my heart, Amy."

"Who says you can? What about your wife and kids?"

"My *what*?!"

"Your wife and kids. What if you wake up tomorrow and remember you have a wife and children who love you and are counting on you to come home. Will it matter then what you've promised me? Even if you're the type of man who could abandon your family to be with me, I could never accept that, or respect you for it."

* * *

Mark sank back, stunned. It had never occurred to him that he might be married and have children. He couldn't possibly be married! Could he? Surely he'd know. Wouldn't his wife have reported him missing by now, if he had one? Wouldn't he have some sense of someone special in his life? There was no way he could feel the way he did about Amy if he were in love with someone else. No way. Was there?

He opened his mouth to speak, and closed it again as he recalled the beautiful brunette with the deep blue eyes who smiled adoringly at him in his dreams. She was just a dream though. Wasn't she? Mark swallowed, hard. What if he *was* married?

Chapter Twenty-Three

Amy was right. He had no way to know for sure. Maybe he travelled a lot and didn't phone much. Maybe they'd had a fight. Maybe she'd reported him missing in some far off place.

He recalled the horrible visions from his nightmares. He couldn't possibly have a wife, could he? With a sinking feeling he realized he couldn't ask Amy to be part of his life either, if that's the way it was. How could he ask her to become part of that? Someone had tried to kill him! He shouldn't even be here, in her home. He was being just as selfish now as David had been years earlier.

Mark noticed Amy still watching him with her large green eyes. They were so lovely. She was so beautiful it hurt to look at her. He couldn't bear the thought of not seeing her again but neither could he allow her to be hurt because of him. He swallowed hard and looked away as he struggled with what to do.

"You're right," he said bleakly. "I can't promise anything until I know who I am. I shouldn't even be here. I've put you at risk long enough."

"God helped me, Mark. Maybe if you asked Him..."

Mark laughed humorlessly. "I wish it were that easy, but I don't think that's going to work for me. I need to figure this out for myself."

"No, you don't. You just need to ask God..."

"Amy! Enough!" Mark snapped, then continued in a softer voice, "Look, I just need some time to think, okay?"

"Sure," she said, a little sadly. "It's about time for me to go to bed anyway. I guess I'll see you in the morning."

Mark nodded silently as Amy uncurled herself from the couch and made her way to the stairs. For once, Bella got up and padded after her instead of staying with him.

She paused at the foot of the stairs. "And Mark? Thank you... for what you did tonight. No one's ever..."

"It's nothing. Don't worry about it," he interrupted before she could finish. He made a pretext of leaning his head back and closing his eyes until she turned to go, then covertly watched as the woman and her dog disappeared up the stairs.

Mark had known from the first that he couldn't stay forever but somehow, over the course of the past few weeks, he had allowed himself to ignore that. Now the truth had him by the heart and was squeezing the life out of him. He would be leaving soon, one way or another, and there was nothing he could do to stop it.

* * *

Amy softly closed the door to her room and padded over to her desk by the window. She sat down where she could see the moon reflecting off the lake far below her as Bella flopped down at her feet. A light wind sighed through the evergreens and roughed up the lake so the moonlight danced and bounced across its surface. It was such a beautiful night, yet she was in no mood to enjoy it. She stared out the window, lost in thought.

Mark had said it was nothing, what he'd done that night, but it wasn't nothing. It was something so big she couldn't quite seem to grasp it. He'd sacrificed his own safety to protect her. Why? What did he get out of it? Nothing. He'd lost his safe place. He had nowhere to go. She hadn't even given him a thank you kiss. So why'd he do it?

Amy replayed the night's events in her mind, trying to remember what Mark had said and how he'd reacted, trying to make some sense of it. Everything jumbled around in her brain. She knew the answer was there, somewhere. It should be obvious, but the more she chased it, the more confused she became.

Finally Amy knelt on the floor, quieted her spirit, and prayed, "Lord, I'm so confused. Please help me understand why he did this. Why?"

Because he loves you.

The thought was so clear in her mind that Amy gasped.

"He loves me? But that can't be true," she muttered aloud. "He's only known me three weeks. That's not enough time.

"And if he does? What am I supposed to do about that? I still don't know who he is or what he's done. Besides, he never said he loved me."

Amy closed her eyes, searching her memory. What he'd done was bring happiness back into her life. He'd laughed with her and noticed when she was sad. He'd kissed her then let her go when she'd pushed him away. He'd cooked for her even when she'd refused to eat and protected her when she'd offered him nothing in return. What he'd done said more about who he was than any biography ever could. His actions spoke more honestly than what mere words would ever convey.

Amy swallowed as a shiver ran through her. "What if he's already married? And if he isn't, Lord, he still doesn't love You. He doesn't even believe in You. I couldn't ever marry him like that." Tears welled in her eyes as the realization of how impossible the situation was threatened to engulf her.

In spite of her best efforts at remaining aloof, the truth was that, whether Mark loved her or not, she had fallen in love with him, deeply and completely. Once again she found herself in love with a man who didn't love God and who was going to leave her in the end. Tears spilled over her cheeks and splashed onto her hands lying clasped tightly in her lap.

If only Mark would believe, would trust in the Lord. "Please help him, Lord. Please help him trust You." She took a shuddering breath, "And please help me accept whatever comes."

There was no answer in the silent room, but somehow Amy felt a peace wash over her. She took a ragged breath in and slowly let it go along with the fear she had been drowning in. It was all she could do.

* * *

Two towns over, a tall, handsome man with perfect blonde hair parked his SUV in the parking lot of the Kicking Horse Saloon. He pushed his way through the door and crossed the grimy floor to a dingy booth in the back corner. The two men already there looked up silently from their conversation and one moved over to make room for the newcomer.

Flagging down the waitress, the blonde man said, "Two beers, honey, and make it quick." He gave her backside a little slap as she went past him. She cast him a filthy look but said nothing as she returned to the bar to fetch his drinks.

Turning back to his companions, the man smiled a slow, malicious smile and said, "I think I've found the guy you've been looking for."

The man with the gold ring smiled coldly as his scarred friend exhaled a thin stream of smoke and crushed out his cigarette.

* * *

The next morning Amy came downstairs to find Mark still sitting on the couch where she'd left him. His hair was standing on end, as if he'd been running his fingers through it and there were dark circles under his eyes.

"More nightmares?" Amy asked, concerned.

Mark shook his head. "Didn't sleep. Been thinking." He rubbed his face with his hands.

"You need to get some sleep," she offered gently, crouching down beside him.

"After I call Dale. I can't stay here anymore," he said bleakly.

Amy's heart sank into the pit of her stomach. Swallowing past the lump in her throat she said, "If that's what you want to do, but I haven't changed my mind. You can stay here as long as you need to."

Mark raised his eyes to hers. He seemed more than just tired. There was an air of defeat about him, like everything he had tried had ended in failure and exhaustion. It wrenched at Amy's heart to see him that way.

Without thinking, she leaned forward and placed a soft, gentle kiss on his lips, lingering only briefly but completely catching him off guard. His eyes widened minutely and a small frown creased his brow.

"Try to get some sleep. I'll be in the clinic if you need me. I'll keep my eyes open and call Dale if anything seems even a little suspicious." She turned and left the room quickly, unwilling to let him see the tears welling in her eyes.

* * *

Mark sat in puzzled silence fingering the lip that still tingled from her kiss. He tried to make some sense of it but was too tired to think. He finally hauled himself up and grabbed the telephone.

"Dale? It's Mark. I shouldn't stay here any longer. I want you to move me. It's not safe for Amy... Tomorrow? Can't we do this today?.. No, I'm not telling you how to do your job... Fine. Tomorrow morning's fine." Mark banged the receiver down a little too harshly. Could nothing work out the way he wanted it to?

Feeling bleary-eyed, he wandered out onto the deck, hoping the chill autumn air would revive him. The wind blew right through his clothes creating goosebumps all over, but his mind remained foggy. He knew he needed sleep, but stubbornly clung to consciousness as he wrestled with his problem. How could he be what Amy needed with no memory and a questionable past? How could he stop the inevitable progression of events that was taking him out of her life forever? He gazed out over the valley as if hoping to find the answers there.

If only there really were a God who could just fix this problem for him like Amy believed. Mark knew it couldn't be that easy though. Life was never easy. The past few weeks sure proved that.

He closed his eyes, desperate for answers but running out of options. It was becoming impossible to think straight.

Finally, weariness overcame him, and he dragged himself up the stairs to his room. Just before he collapsed into an exhausted, fitful sleep he thought, if only there really were a God.

Wouldn't it be nice if she were right?

Chapter Twenty-Four

That night Amy jolted awake from a deep sleep. She lay in bed silently, eyes wide and heart racing, listening. Listening. All was quiet.

Bella lay by her bed snoring softly. Amy let her breath out in a soft rush. Whatever had awakened her couldn't have been too serious or the dog would be barking instead of sleeping. The clock by her bed read 1:00 a.m. Something had awoken her, but what? Maybe Mark had had another nightmare. Wide awake now anyway, Amy quietly got up and padded down the hall to peek into his room.

Sure enough, she found him sitting up in bed, elbows braced on bent knees and head in his hands. The moonlight filtered in the window, illuminating his bare chest and shoulders. He ran a shaky hand through his hair as he looked up, finally noticing her scrutiny.

"Are you okay?"she asked softly.

* * *

"Yeah, fine. It's nothing. Go back to sleep," he said wearily, despising the slight tremor in his voice.

Mark looked away from her, out the window. Why didn't she leave? He hated for her to see him like this, shaking like a child, afraid of shadows in the dark. An intense wave of gratitude flooded through him though, when she ignored his instructions to go and came over to sit by him instead.

Amy slid a pajama-clad arm around his shoulders as she asked, "Want to talk about it? It might help."

He shook his head. "It's just fragments, nothing that makes sense." He didn't tell her how bloody and violent those fragments were. The dead vacant eyes of the beautiful couple stared back at him from the shadows of his mind.

They sat like that for a long while, side by side with her arm around him. He kept his eyes closed, allowing the warmth from her body to penetrate him. Slowly the hammering of his heart calmed and the tension eased from his shoulders as the images in his mind faded into the background once more.

Moonlight streamed in the window, bathing everything in silver light. Somewhere in the distance an owl hooted, soft and low, as if greeting its mate. The night had a magical feel to it, like a scene from *A Midsummer Night's Dream*. They sat in silence.

Mark's mind had turned from the terrors in his dreams to the beautiful woman sitting so close beside him. He wanted nothing more in that moment, than to enfold her in his arms, lay her down, and kiss her until all his demons were pushed away into the far recesses of his subconscious. He wanted to lose himself completely in the warmth of her body, the fragrance of her skin, and the sweet fullness of her lips. The need to hold her was so strong it burned inside him, yet he knew he couldn't. She wouldn't allow it.

As if reading his mind, Amy stood up and said, "I should go now."

"Don't," he pleaded softly, catching her hand before she could turn to leave.

She looked like a frightened fawn in the moonlight, all honey blonde hair and huge luminous eyes.

"Please... just lie here beside me awhile longer, on top of the covers. No funny business... I promise." His eyes added 'don't make me beg.'

Amy hesitated. He could see in her eyes she longed to do more than just lie down beside him but he read fear there, too. His heart sank as she turned away, but she surprised him by grabbing a spare blanket off the chair and wrapping it around herself.

"Just for a little while. No funny business," she repeated softly.

Mark slid down under the covers lying face up while she lay on top of them, beside him, her head resting on his shoulder. Her nearness had his heart pounding again, but if she noticed, she didn't say. Soon he could tell from her slow, deep breathing that she was asleep.

He marveled at her trust in him. Here he was, a potentially dangerous person, yet she felt safe enough to fall asleep in his arms. He turned his face towards her and gently kissed her forehead, breathing in the perfume of her hair.

He still couldn't remember his old life but he doubted it was much like this: warm, safe, happy. From the fragments of nightmare he recalled, he guessed his real life was violent and lonely. He didn't want to go back. He didn't want to remember if it meant losing all this.

The ache in his chest warned him he probably had no choice. This little piece of heaven he'd awoken to was only an illusion that couldn't last. His past would hunt him down eventually, literally.

What kind of person was he? The contrasts between the stuff in his dreams and the way he felt with Amy were driving him crazy. He didn't think he was a bad person. He didn't feel evil. Yet the images he saw at night told a completely different story. He was convinced he had either seen or done terrible things.

Mark stared bleakly up at the ceiling as his arm tightened around Amy's shoulders. She made a sleepy little sound, sighed deeply and snuggled in closer to him, draping one arm across his chest.

It was exquisite torture. He wanted her so badly it hurt. Yet, in the torment of the moment, he discovered something about himself. He was a man of his word. He'd promised her no funny business and he'd honor that, even if it killed him.

Here was the catch that was eating him alive. He wanted her in his life forever, completely, wholly, not just the one-night stand she was afraid of, but without his memory he had nothing to offer her, not even a name. He couldn't even promise there was no one else in his life. He didn't know. To keep her, he had to remember, but if he remembered, he could lose her forever.

There was also the fact that his just being here could be placing her in danger. He could never live with himself if something happened to her because of him.

He needed to remember. He had to, but he didn't want to. He was afraid of what he'd find. He was so confused, and there was no one who could help him. Not one single person. He'd never felt as alone as he did at that moment.

Mark turned his mind back towards Amy. She had said she was never alone and never without hope. She had called Jesus her rock and her best friend.

God.

Could there really be a God out there? One who cared and could actually do something? Amy said God loved him and wanted to help. He was just waiting for Mark to ask.

Mark felt a longing so deep and so strong in his soul. If only that were true. If only there really was a God who loved him and could help. If only...

Mark lay on his back, staring at the ceiling for a long time, agonizing. It couldn't possibly be true, could it?

Finally, longing and need overpowered stubbornness and doubt. With silent tears creeping from the corners of his eyes, Mark spoke quietly into the darkness.

"God? If You're really out there... I... I need help. I can't do this alone. Please... The things I see in my dreams... If I've really done that, I'm sorry. Please help me remember who I am. If I really am an evil person, I'm going to need Your help to change that. Please... I don't want to lose Amy. God.... Are you there? I need You."

When he finished praying, Mark let the silence of the room engulf him. The only sound was Amy's soft breathing.

He wasn't sure what he'd expected, if anything, but his memories didn't flash back into his mind like someone turning a movie on. God didn't suddenly speak in a booming voice from out of nowhere. There were no words on the wall or a burning bush.

What did happen was much more subtle but just as miraculous. The fear and anxiety which had been strangling his heart loosened their grip and were slowly pushed aside by a growing sense of peace. Mark brushed the tears from his face and turned to study Amy. She slept peacefully on his shoulder.

Joy welled up within him to the point where he almost laughed. So that's where it came from. This peace he was feeling now, it was the same peace that carried her through all this turmoil and kept her steady. It was from God. It was His presence. He really was there!

Then Mark did laugh, quietly. He still couldn't remember but he knew, somehow, that everything would be all right. He wasn't alone anymore.

He gazed at Amy nestled so sweetly beside him. With his free hand he brushed a few stray locks of hair off her face.

"I love you," he whispered gently.

In her sleep, Amy smiled, almost as if she'd heard him. Mark closed his eyes with a sigh and was soon deeply, peacefully asleep. And for once, there were no nightmares to haunt him.

When he awoke in the early dawn light, he remembered everything. He turned his eyes to the woman sleeping peacefully beside him. No wonder the name Mark had sounded so comfortable on her lips. It was just like his real name, Marc with a 'C', short for Marcus. He kissed her gently on the forehead before sliding from the bed, grabbing his clothes, and slipping silently out the door.

Chapter Twenty-Five

Amy's eyes lazily fluttered open and she lay for a moment of drowsy contentment, clinging to the last vestiges of sleep. She'd been enjoying the most wonderful dream about her and Mark. With a slow sinking feeling the truth came back to her, however. Mark was leaving today, and she'd probably never see him again. Amy sighed a deep long sigh and rolled over.

Having become frustrated with the lack of progress he was making on the investigation, and being pushed by Mark to move him, Dale had reluctantly agreed to transfer Mark to the city police department and let them take over the investigation. They had the manpower to keep Mark safe until they figured out who he was. They might also have better connections to pull some strings and get some answers. Dale was due to pick Mark up at 10:00 a.m.

Amy had to admit it was a better plan than keeping Mark hidden at her place. In the city he could get some decent medical help and might stand a better chance of regaining his memory. She and Dale should have moved Mark a couple of weeks ago, as soon as he was well enough, instead of waiting. Then maybe she wouldn't be feeling quite as desolate as she did right now.

Amy blinked and looked around the room, finally realizing she was in Mark's room, not her own. She must have fallen asleep beside him last night. Amy sat up. She was still fully clad in her pajamas and wrapped in the spare blanket.

There was no sign of Mark anywhere.

He must be downstairs, she thought as she got up and disappeared into her bedroom to shower and change.

Amy dawdled getting ready. She was anxious to spend the last couple of hours with Mark, but dreading finally having to say good-bye. What if she completely humiliated herself by crying? What good would that do? There was no point in making him feel bad when, in all likelihood, there was no hope for a real relationship out of all this anyway.

She dressed casually but carefully in a fitted pair of jeans that accentuated her curves nicely and a stretch green print T-shirt that picked up the color of her eyes and complemented her skin tone perfectly. She added a touch of perfume and hint of lipstick and eye makeup, making sure the mascara was waterproof, just in case.

Finally, she felt ready. Painting on a bright smile to hide her feelings, Amy came down the stairs.

"Mark?"

The living room was silent and empty. Bella stood on the porch looking in through the glass doors, her tail slowly waving like a flag. Mark must have put her out, Amy thought.

"Mark!" Amy called again, louder, as she crossed the room to let Bella in.

There was no response. She walked out onto the porch and scanned her back yard but there was no sign of him there either. Frowning, Amy came back in and went to look out her kitchen window towards the front parking lot. To her great surprise, her old truck was missing.

"What the...." Amy looked to where she always kept her keys on a hook by the door only to find them missing, too.

Amy checked the door and found it still locked securely. There were no signs of broken glass or forced entry either. Whoever took the truck had the keys, and got them without breaking in. Could Mark have taken them?

"Mark!" she bellowed into the silence, no longer really expecting a reply.

With growing confusion, Amy went back into her living room to check the door to the clinic. It was still locked also.

It had to have been Mark. Bella would have barked if anyone else had come in. It was the only reasonable explanation.

Her scowl deepened as anger began to set in. She'd gone to all the trouble to get pretty and spend the last few hours with him and he wasn't even here? What was he doing, taking her truck without asking and disappearing when Dale was due to pick him up soon? What was he thinking?

Then it hit her with sickening clarity. Amy slowly sank down into the armchair as the horrible thought forced its way into her mind. She began to tremble as she searched for any other possible explanation. She could find none.

He had left. He had stolen her truck and taken off before Dale could come and get him. He hadn't even said good-bye. He'd just...left.

Amy struggled just to breathe as the weight of that realization crushed down on her. It had all been lies, everything he'd said about not walking out the way David had. All lies. And now he was gone.

How could she have believed him? It was happening all over again. She had even seen it coming and had walked right into it anyway.

"I... am... so... stupid," she choked into the empty silence.

Bella whined softly and put her head in Amy's lap, looking up mournfully with her big soulful brown eyes. Amy stroked her soft fur automatically as she stared out into space, seeing nothing, feeling numb. She couldn't believe it. How could she have been so wrong about Mark?

There must be some other explanation, she thought desperately.

She was so lost in her own misery that she didn't notice when Bella perked her head up , then ran into the kitchen, put her paws up on the counter and looked out the window. She didn't notice the low growl as all the hair stood up along Bella's back. Nothing got through to her until she heard a thump and a muffled oath from behind the door to the clinic.

Mark? Hope struggled to push back despair. Maybe she'd been wrong. Maybe he'd just needed to do something before Dale arrived and didn't want to wake her. Maybe she was all upset for nothing.

Amy bounced up, unlocked the clinic door and flung it open. "Mark?"

Amy froze. Instead of finding Mark, she found herself looking down the barrel of a handgun pointed straight at her face. It was held by the scruffy blonde man with the scar and tattoos she'd seen weeks earlier in town. His dark-haired buddy loomed just behind him.

"Surprise," the dark one drawled slowly as a malicious smile spread across his wide, ugly face.

Suddenly Bella was there, forcing her way past Amy and barking so ferociously that her teeth clacked together.

Bits of spittle flew from the dog's muzzle as both men startled backwards.

The man with the gun swung it towards Bella and snarled, "Shut that dog up or I'll shoot it!"

"No!" Amy cried, snatching at Bella's collar and dragging her back. "Don't hurt her! I'll lock her up. Please!"

"Get on with it then!" the dark haired man snapped at her. To his friend he said, "Reese! Keep the gun on her while I check the house."

He disappeared into her house while Reese followed Amy as she dragged Bella, still barking and snarling, over to one of the large dog crates in the surgery. Amy shoved Bella into the crate and struggled to latch the door with hands that wouldn't stop shaking.

"Shh, Bella. It's okay," she said in a quavering voice as she crouched beside the crate.

"C'mon!" Reese snapped as he grabbed her arm and hauled her to her feet. Shoving her ahead of him, he directed her back into her house. "Bruno!" he bellowed.

"Right here! Quit yelling," Bruno replied, coming back down the stairs.

"Where do you want her?"

"Here." Bruno grabbed a chair from the kitchen and dragged it into the living room where he positioned it angled towards both the door to the clinic and to the kitchen.

"Sit!" Reese ordered, shoving Amy towards the chair.

She stumbled forward and sat, clasping her hands tightly together in her lap. She kept her eyes down, fearful of doing or saying the wrong thing.

"Where is he?" Bruno barked.

"W-Who?" Amy stammered.

Bruno smiled, but it wasn't pleasant. "*Mark,* or whatever he's calling himself these days."

Amy thought frantically. "Uh... Mark's my cat. When I opened the door and called Mark, I thought you were my..."

"Cut the crap! Jansen already told us he was here," Bruno interjected. "The only question is, where is he *now*?"

Amy's eyes had widened dramatically at the mention of David's last name. That's right! These two were supposedly friends of his. Amy swallowed hard. There was no point in pretending. They already knew and, by the looks of them, they were becoming annoyed by her stalling.

"I...I don't know. He t-took my truck this morning and left. I think he's run off. You missed him." Amy found herself desperately hoping this was true. Then at least Mark would be safe, even if he was a jerk.

Bruno was scowling fiercely. "Was there any kind of car out there when we arrived?" he snapped at Reese.

Reese shook his head.

"Dammit! You'd better not be lying!" he snarled at Amy who flinched back from his anger. Directing his words at Reese he yelled, "Get upstairs and look around. See if you can find any hint where he might have gone."

Reese disappeared up the stairs as Bruno began searching around her living room, ruffling through papers on the desk and generally making a mess. He cursed and knocked things to the floor in his efforts but didn't seem to know what he should be looking for.

Amy sat paralyzed in her chair, afraid to move. She briefly considered making a run for the door but, even if she made it outside, then what? Her neighbors were all too far away for her to run to easily. She hadn't seen if Bruno had a gun or not, but even if he didn't, she didn't think he'd need one to break her neck. All she could do was sit and pray they got tired of this and left. Please, God, please!

At least Mark was safe, she thought ruefully. Even if he was a lying, back-stabbing scumbag thief she couldn't bear the thought of these two getting their hands on him.

Barely five minutes later Reese's boots thundered back down the stairs. He had a big, ugly grin on his face. "Look what I found on the floor in the bedroom." He shoved an 8 by 11 inch sheet of paper into Bruno's hand.

Bruno began to read aloud. "Amy. Gone to talk to Dale. Be back soon. Mark." He began to chuckle nastily.

"Well, ain't that convenient? He's coming right back here and he left us a note so we wouldn't worry 'bout him."

Amy's head was spinning. She didn't know whether to laugh or cry. Mark hadn't stolen her truck and run off after all! He'd left a great big note for her to find right on the bed. Somehow, it must have fallen to the floor and she hadn't even seen it when she got up. He was coming back, right into a trap, and she had no way to warn him.

"Here!" Bruno tossed a roll of duct tape towards Reese who caught it. "Tie her to the chair and tape her mouth. I want him to get a real good look at her when he comes through the door. Then we'll surprise him real good."

Both men began to laugh as Bruno pulled out a large semiautomatic handgun from inside his jacket, checked the magazine, and closed it with a snap. Reese pulled Amy's hands back behind the chair and began wrapping them with tape. She grimaced with the pain that shot up her arm and felt a couple of teardrops slide down her face. He taped each of her ankles to the chair legs and wrapped another loop several times around her waist.

Mark didn't stand a chance.

Chapter Twenty-Six

Marcus drove impatiently down the highway towards Amy's place. He swerved out into oncoming traffic briefly to see if he could pass the slow-moving truck in front of him but there were cars approaching so he had to retreat back behind the truck. He cursed under his breath, feeling a twinge of guilt because of his newfound relationship with God. He glanced up, under his eyebrows, towards Heaven. "Sorry," he mumbled and continued driving.

Explaining everything to Dale had taken much longer than he had anticipated.

Of course, Marc had arrived at the station well before Dale was usually there, so he'd had to drive across town to the sheriff's home to pound on his door. Not surprisingly, Dale had been less than amused at being woken so early. It had taken a lot of persuasion from Marc to get him to agree to go down to the station immediately, and then it'd taken another twenty minutes for him to get ready and actually leave.

Marc was grinding his teeth by the time they finally got to the station, and then Dale threw up another roadblock. He refused to release Marc's gun to him until he checked his story out. Even after Marc had produced all his credentials from the hidden compartment in his car, Dale had insisted he needed to speak to Marc's supervisor personally. It had taken forever to track the man down and get him to confirm all the details.

Marc swerved out to peek past the truck in front of him and just as quickly swerved back to avoid being hit. Where was all this traffic coming from so early on a Saturday morning? He glanced down at his watch. 9:30 a.m. What should have taken him forty-five minutes to an hour at the most had stretched into nearly three and a half hours.

Marc ran a hand through his hair and mentally berated himself. He should have woken Amy and taken her with him instead of leaving her home alone. If he'd known it was going to take this long...

Marc took a deep breath and forced himself to calm down. Amy was fine, he assured himself. They'd been fine for three and a half weeks so far and she'd be fine for a few hours alone, certainly. He was just overreacting from the adrenaline rush of remembering his life.

Finally, Marc pulled into the clinic parking lot in a cloud of dust. He barely noticed the black sedan parked on the other side of the road, assuming it belonged to one of the neighboring houses. He climbed from the truck, tucked his gun into the waist of his pants, and strode over to the door to the kitchen.

He noted with irritation that his limp was a little more pronounced after three hours of walking and driving than it had been earlier. All in all though, his leg had been improving steadily. Amy seemed to have done an excellent job stitching him up. He briefly touched the spot on his forehead where he'd hit his head. There was barely a mark left to indicate anything had ever happened. It would be interesting to see what a real doctor would have to say about the results when he finally got it checked out.

Marc opened the door and strode into the kitchen as he called out, "Amy!"

He stopped dead in his tracks.

His heart stuttered the moment he saw her through the door to the living room, duct taped to the chair with her eyes wide and frightened.

It was a trap.

He reached for his weapon, but too late. Marc felt the cold, hard muzzle of a gun pressed to the back of his neck.

"Don't move," said a low, ominous voice from behind him.

Marc froze, then slowly raised his hands to shoulder height. Fear and fury clenched his gut as he saw the tear stains on Amy's face. She was terrified and it was he who had brought all of this down on top of her. His mind blanked for a moment as their eyes met.

If she died...

Summoning years of training and experience, Marc tore his eyes away from her. He had to think. He had to stay calm and in control if they were to have any chance at all. He couldn't allow himself to be paralyzed with fear over her safety. He pushed Amy completely from his mind and forced himself back into the persona he'd been using for over a year. He wasn't sure if these were the same guys who'd tampered with his brakes or not. Maybe, if he was really lucky, they were out of the loop and still believed he was one of them.

Marc relaxed his stance, dropping his arms slightly, and painted a smile on his face. "Bruno, is that you?" he asked.

Bruno stepped into view beside Amy, pistol held casually pointed in her direction. "We've been lookin' all over fer you, Tanner."

"So that must be Reese behind me then?"

Reese grunted his acknowledgement. Bruno continued to point his gun in Amy's direction. He watched Marc intently, a smug, slightly amused expression on his face. He had small, piggy eyes set deeply in a wide face on a thick, almost non-existent neck attached to massive shoulders. He looked like he should have the IQ of a turnip, but Marc knew behind his outward bulk lay a cold, calculating mind with a cruel streak and a short fuse. Reese, on the other hand, really wasn't the brightest bulb on the Christmas tree, but he knew how to follow orders which made him a reliable flunky.

"What took you guys so long?" Marc complained. "I've been waiting for over three weeks since my car went off the road. I had to hide out in this dumpy place so the cops wouldn't see me. I couldn't even go to the hospital for stitches. And what's with the damn guns, huh? Put them down. We're all friends, ain't we?"

Bruno barked with laughter at that, quickly followed by Reese who gouged the gun painfully into the base of Marc's neck. Marc felt what little hope he'd had begin to dissipate as Bruno's laughter faded and his eyes hardened to a cold glare.

"Friends?" Bruno repeated with an unpleasant sneer. "Is that what we are, Tanner? Or is it Mark now? Or could it really be Marcus? As in Agent Marcus Taylor of the DEA?"

Behind her duct tape, Amy squeaked in surprise and her eyes grew wide. Bruno, noticing this, began to chuckle nastily.

"Whatsa matter, sweetheart? Good old Tanner here not tell you about how he's been pretending to be our friend for over a year while planning to stab us in the back the whole time?" Bruno sneered. "It's a good thing the boss found out about him or he could have caused a lot of trouble."

Marc swallowed reflexively.

They knew everything.

He straightened his stance, keeping a mask of arrogant confidence on his face. Outwardly he hoped he appeared calm and collected. Inwardly, he was frantically trying to think of any way out of this mess. He flipped though scenario after scenario of possible escape plans, each one more ludicrous and impossible than the last. He refused to allow himself to look at Amy, knowing if he did, he'd fall apart completely.

It would be so much easier if it weren't for Amy. Even a month ago he would have viewed this situation as a minor inconvenience. He would have spun to face Reese, shoving his gun aside with one hand while smashing Reese in the face with the other, then using Reese as a shield, would have shot Bruno before he had a chance to blink. It would have been highly risky, but that was all part of the job. And if he'd died trying, well, then he'd have gone out the way he'd lived: hard, fast and alone.

Amy changed everything.

He couldn't put her in further danger by one of his wild stunts, and for once, he actually had a reason to want to stay alive himself. He had to come up with a way out that kept her safe.

"Enough chit-chat between old friends. You!" Bruno ordered, pointing his gun at Marc, "get over here beside your girlfriend!"

"She's not my girlfriend!" Marc snapped harshly.

"Whatever!" Reese grumbled as he shoved Marc forward with the muzzle of his gun.

Marc reluctantly crossed the room to where Bruno still stood beside Amy. Marc's eyes met Bruno's as he approached, and it took every ounce of control he possessed not to slam his fist right into Bruno's mouth, erasing his smug expression. If he could have done it without risking Amy he would have, and damn the consequences. Bruno seemed to almost read his mind as he smirked even more, daring Marc to try something foolish. Marc kept his face neutral, but his eyes flashed dangerously as he stopped right in front of Bruno. He could still feel Reese breathing down his back.

Bruno slowly reached around Marc's back and withdrew the gun hidden there, tossing it casually to the floor away from them. Marc watched helplessly as his last hope skittered across the floor to stop some twelve feet away. Bruno shoved Marc closer to Amy's chair and moved over to stand beside Reese.

"You know, it's a shame you didn't just die in that accident like you were supposed to." Bruno snarled maliciously. "Now we're going to have to kill both you and the girl."

"Leave her out of it!" Mark said, trying to keep his voice even. "She doesn't know anything."

"She knows enough! She's seen both of us, knows our names, and she knows Jansen's part of it," Bruno countered. "Besides, we got our orders. Kill you. Leave no witnesses."

"You're too late then," Marc said, feigning confidence. "I just got back from the Sheriff's office and he knows everything. He's seen the two of you and he knows you're with Jansen. He's due to show up here any minute. The best thing you boys could do would be to pack it up and get out of here as fast as you can before you get caught."

"Oh, we will. We will." Bruno chortled. "Right after we kill you and burn this whole place down. And I wouldn't be holding my breath waiting for that dumb old sheriff if I was you." Bruno glanced down at his watch. "Jansen was due to stage a robbery at the liquor store about twenty minutes ago. When that dopey sheriff shows up, I'm afraid he just might get shot, too. Like I said, no witnesses."

* * *

Behind her duct tape Amy tried to scream "No!" and began wrenching at her bonds. The tape held more securely than any rope ever would have. She looked up at Marc standing to her left. He stood motionless and stone-faced as he stared down their assailants. He seemed so calm, just like the other night with David, but the pulse at the base of his throat said otherwise.

She had been praying non-stop for divine help since these two ruffians had burst into her home. She had been praying for Marc, too. Now, she looked up at him to see what he might do to get them out of this.

* * *

Beside her, Marc finally allowed himself to glance down at her again. He was expecting to see tears and terror but instead he found two great big green eyes watching him expectantly, filled with hope and trust. He tore his eyes quickly away and swallowed hard as panic surged through his veins. She thought he could still get them out of this, but he had nothing! He'd played his last card and had no more tucked up his sleeve.

Marc was dimly aware of Reese and Bruno arguing over whether Jansen was going to get this assignment right or mess up again, and whether he and Amy should be killed first or allowed to die in the fire. He was acutely aware that Amy was still watching him expectantly. His mind searched frantically for a way out but he came up blank. He was out of ideas and out of hope.

Marc closed his eyes. She was going to die, just like his parents had, and he alone was responsible.

He alone.

Out of hope.

Never alone. Never without hope.

Marc's eyes flew open as the words hit his mind like a sledge hammer. They had been so clear, so solid, as if someone had spoken aloud, yet there had been no actual sound. His pulse began to race. Amy had told him about this! Could it actually be God?

God! How could he have forgotten so quickly? He wasn't alone anymore. He'd asked God into his life just last night. But could God actually do anything to help? There was only one way to find out.

Marc closed his eyes again and began to pray silently. *God? You gave my memory back when I asked. I don't know if You can do anything about this but I really need Your help again. Please give me some idea to get us out of this. I'll die if I have to but please help me save Amy!*

Marc stopped and waited, holding his breath. Amy had told him sometimes you had to wait for an answer. He forcibly calmed his mind. Hopefully God wouldn't take too long to answer as Bruno and Reese's discussion seemed to be winding down.

Suddenly a picture came to his mind of how he might get them both out of trouble. It was totally wild and completely risky.

Marc scowled and prayed back, silently. *Lord! You've got to be kidding! That's worse than some of the stuff I came up with. Maybe if I was in top shape, it might work, but I still can't even walk without limping. How can You expect me to pull this off?*

Marc held his breath.

Trust me.

Well, that was it then, wasn't it? He either believed God or he didn't. He either trusted God and obeyed Him, or he didn't. Time to make up his mind.

"Enough talk!" Bruno barked. "We shoot them first, put them in the kitchen, then blow the gas line. That's final! Reese, stand over by the kitchen so you can watch the door but keep your gun on Tanner. If he moves, shoot him! I want to watch his face as I shoot his li'l gal here. Then we do him and we're outta here."

As Bruno raised his gun, Marc moved. In one fluid motion, as if he'd never been hurt, Marc launched himself into the air and kicked Amy hard near her shoulder, toppling her chair over sideways with a crash, and launching himself in the other direction towards his gun still lying on the floor. Marc heard Bruno's gun go off as he kicked, followed instantly by Reese's. He felt the bullet whiz by his head as he hit the floor, grabbed his gun, rolled into position, and fired two rounds in rapid succession. Bruno, then Reese, hit the floor almost simultaneously.

Chapter Twenty-Seven

Marc remained lying on the floor panting, waiting, watching for any movement or sign of counterattack. The loud tick of the wall clock reverberated with the pounding of his heart in his ears. Nothing moved.

He got up and scrambled over to Bruno. Dead. Marc took Bruno's gun anyway and tossed it across the room. Then he checked Reese. Not dead yet, but soon. Very soon. Marc took that gun and tossed it, too. Reese emitted one last gurgling sigh and was gone. Marc shuddered. He'd seen far too much of that.

Having made sure all threats were neutralized, Marc finally turned his attention towards Amy. She'd been so quiet. Eerily quiet. He looked to where she'd landed only moments before, and what met his eyes knocked the wind out of him. She lay perfectly still on her side, still taped to the chair, blood turning her blonde hair crimson.

"No!" Marc roared, stumbling forward and dropping to his knees beside her silent form.

"No...." His voice cracked as he reached out with a shaking hand to gently sweep a tendril of hair off her face. He could hardly breathe, as if an invisible hand had crushed his heart beyond its ability to beat. He closed his eyes, sucking air, shaking.

"No, God, no. Me... Not her. Please not her." The words came out like broken shards of glass.

Marc's mind raced in an incoherent mess, but finally reverted back to years of ingrained training. He lurched to his feet, strode to the kitchen, and dialed 9-1-1. He immediately abandoned the phone on the counter, knowing help would come when he failed to respond to the operator. He grabbed a paring knife out of the drawer, and hurried back to Amy's side. In only a few seconds he had cut her bonds and laid her flat.

Kneeling beside her, Marc gently placed his fingers along her throat, feeling for a pulse. She was so pale... He felt nothing, but his hand was shaking so badly he couldn't be sure.

Check... breathing. Marc had to force himself to follow his first aid training.

Amy's mouth was still taped shut. He couldn't feel any air. He fumbled with the tape, finally snagging the edge, and pulled it off. Then he waited, hovering over her, not daring to breathe himself. He could hear the clock. One second. Two seconds. Three.

At five seconds, her chest rose in a faint little breath. Marc released his own breath in a sob of relief. Knowing it was wrong to move her, but unable to help himself, Marc scooped her up and held her close against his chest. Rocking gently, her head resting against his chest, he murmured into her hair, "I'm so sorry, Amy. This is all my fault. I'll never let you be hurt again. I swear. Please, don't leave me. I love you. Please, don't leave me. Please..."

* * *

Dimly, Amy became aware of words floating through her mind.

"… don't leave me… love you..."

Who was going to leave, she wondered fuzzily. She seemed to be rocking back and forth, warm and cozy. Her mind drifted briefly, resting on the soft murmur of words and, beneath it, the strong steady thump of a heartbeat. Slowly, the voice became familiar. Marc's strong tones floated through her head, calm and comforting. What was he saying? What was going on? Amy struggled back to the surface.

"Marc?" she breathed. The rocking stopped abruptly. She felt the arms around her shift and Marc's face drifted in front of her.

"Amy?" he choked. "Amy, speak to me. Are you okay?"

Amy's focus solidified and she saw the fear in his eyes, the moisture on his cheeks. "What happened?" she mumbled, still confused.

"They shot at you, sweetheart, but it's okay. I got them. They can't hurt you anymore." His voice broke at the last, and he crushed her against his chest once more.

"I'm fine. Really, I am," she said softly. At least she thought she was. Her head was aching but aside from that, nothing seemed to hurt. She was a little fuzzy about all the details, but she was beginning to recall the morning's events. Last thing she remembered, Bruno had been one second away from shooting her. Somehow, Marc had saved them both and was holding her now like he'd never let go. She could feel his heart pounding still, under her cheek.

Amy had to repeat her assurances a few more times before Marc released his hold and eased her back onto the floor. As he leaned back, rubbing a hand across his face, she noticed the big red stain on his shirt. "Marc! You're bleeding!" she gasped.

He glanced down surprised. "This?" He pulled his shirt away from his body. "This isn't mine," he mumbled not meeting her gaze. "It's yours. Your hair's covered in blood. Don't move. I'll get a cloth."

Amy watched him stride to the bathroom. She reached up and prodded gently at her head where it hurt. Marc returned a moment later.

"Look at this," Amy said, pulling back part of her hair. "I think I've cut myself."

Marc gently pulled her hair back , revealing a long laceration across her scalp where Bruno's bullet had barely missed its mark. He looked grim as he muttered, "The bullet just grazed you." He pressed the cloth to her scalp as he cradled the opposite side of her face with his other hand.

Amy lay still, her hands on her chest, just watching him. Finally she said, "Are you sure you're okay? You look awfully pale."

Marc cracked a lopsided smile. "Yeah. I'll be fine. I'm used to this, remember? I hang out with drug dealers and gangs all the time."

"So you *are* with the DEA?"

"Marcus Taylor, at your service."

"Marcus." She rolled the word off her tongue, getting a feel for it.

"My friends just call me Marc."

"So your name really is Marc? Weird." She thought for a moment. "Maybe that's why you picked 'Mark' when I suggested the names." She paused, then asked, "If you're DEA why didn't Dale find your picture in their data base?"

Marc sighed. "I've been undercover trying to infiltrate this drug gang for the last eighteen months. The DEA erased my identity. Some of these gangs have a long reach and have access to those data bases. We had to make sure that if they went looking for me they'd come up with nothing."

"Just like Dale did."

"Right. Just like Dale did."

"So that explains the VIN on the car and the registration number on the gun, too."

"And why no one was looking for me. They were used to me dropping off the grid from time to time. They had just started getting worried last week when I'd been out of contact for too long."

"What about the nightmares? DEA stuff?"

"Yeah, mostly." Marc glanced away, not meeting her eyes.

"What about those people you told me about? The couple that always died?"

"They were my parents." Marc hesitated. "They died in a car accident when I was a teenager."

"Oh," Amy said lamely. "I'm sorry."

"It was a long time ago," Marc answered quietly.

In the distance, the faint wail of sirens could be heard approaching. Amy watched as Marc glanced over his shoulder towards the door. Her eyes drank in every ounce of him, from the tiny pink line where she'd stitched his forehead, to the shadow of whiskers on the sharp angle of his jaw, to the muscle and sinew of his neck where they flowed into the wide expanse of his shoulders and chest.

She wished she had let him kiss her before, when he'd wanted to. Now their time together was almost over, and it was too late.

There was only one other burning question on her mind, but she was afraid to ask. Instead she said, "What were you doing up the Lake Road?"

"When David joined the gang, they started making regular trips out here. I did some investigating and found out David's grandfather had an old cabin up the mountain. I was pretty sure they were making meth up there. I was on my way to check it out when my brakes blew out. What I don't understand is why David would come to your clinic and stir up trouble. He should have been trying to keep a low profile instead of drawing attention to himself."

Amy closed her eyes a moment. "That's because you underestimate his huge ego. He probably thought he could walk back into my life, and I'd be so grateful to have him back, that I'd agree to anything. He may have thought I'd even let him sell his stuff out of my clinic."

"He's that delusional?"

"Possibly." Amy smiled ruefully. "So when did you remember?"

"Early this morning. I prayed about it last night and, when I woke up, I remembered everything. I thought I could sneak out and get my gun and be back before you woke up, but it took way longer than I'd expected. I'm sorry, Amy. I should never have left you here alone. This was all my fault."

Amy heard him but it was his first words which grabbed her attention. "You? Prayed?"

Marc grinned, sheepishly. "Yeah. I'd completely run out of options. It was the only thing I hadn't tried yet. It worked though! I guess maybe there really is a God after all."

Amy's smile radiated pure joy. "Oh Marc! God really does love you." And so do I, she wanted to add, but couldn't bring herself to voice it.

The sirens were getting closer.

He was looking at her so tenderly, still cupping her face between his hands as he held the cloth to her head. His eyes seemed locked to her face, as if trying to memorize every curve, every angle. Amy struggled to ask the only question that still tormented her: What about your wife and kids? She couldn't force herself to speak the question.

The sadness in his eyes told her everything she didn't want to know. He was leaving. She swallowed back the pain that flooded over her. Marc looked back over his shoulder again as the sirens stopped outside.

A familiar voice bellowed, "Amy!" The door slammed open and Dale strode into the kitchen.

"In here!" Marc called out.

"Dale!" Amy's voice broke in relief. "You're okay!"

"Course I am." Dale paused at the door and surveyed the living room, noting the two bodies and Marc still kneeling beside Amy on the floor. "What'd you think?"

"Those two said David was faking a liquor store holdup as an excuse to shoot you."

"He tried. Didn't work." Dale looked almost amused. "I may be an old dog, but I still know a few new tricks. Jansen thinks he's so smart that he underestimates everyone else. I saw him coming a mile away. He's cooling his heels back in lock-up right now."

Dale had crossed the room and knelt beside Amy and Marc. "How you doing, Amy girl?" His usually gruff voice became soft and husky all of a sudden.

"I'm fine, really. It's just a scalp wound." She offered Dale what she hoped was a reassuring smile. She couldn't let either man see how badly her heart was breaking at this moment. It would be too humiliating to admit to Dale that he'd been right about her after all her protests vowing she didn't love Marc. As for Marc, he didn't have to say there was no room in his life for her. She'd told herself over and over that he had his own life and as soon as he remembered it he would be gone. It was her own fault if she'd allowed her imagination to think otherwise.

The ambulance attendants arrived and shouldered Marc and Dale out of the way as they went to tend to Amy.

"Bullet barely missed her," Marc muttered softly to Dale as they stood and moved to the other side of the room. "I almost got her killed. An inch further over and ...."

Amy watched as the two men she cared about most drifted out of earshot.

* * *

Dale scowled ferociously. "You two! " he bellowed over to the attendants. "You take good care of that girl but don't touch nothin' else! My men need to get in here and take some pictures and I don't want stuff getting moved around before they do." Turning towards Marc, he added, "I'll follow you and Amy down to the hospital and get statements from you there."

"I'm not going to the hospital," Mark said flatly, keeping his face expressionless. He stood with his arms crossed. He was facing Dale but his eyes slid right past him to rest on Amy. They clung to her face, memorizing every angle of nose and jaw, the soft curve of her cheek, the delicate arch of her brow and the flash of emerald in her eyes.

"You're not?"

"No." He wrenched his gaze back towards Dale.

Dale scowled. "I thought you cared about this girl."

"I do. That's why I'm not going. I can't be seen with her. If the wrong people find out how much I care about her, they could come after her to get to me. No one can know, Dale, not even Amy. She won't be safe.

I'll make a statement down at the station, then I'm heading back to my own home base. There's a lot of work left to do before this case is done."

"Why can't Amy know?" Dale asked gruffly. "She's a smart gal. She'll keep it quiet."

"What if she doesn't?" Marc retorted. "What if she calls too often? Lets it slip to the wrong person? I can't risk it. Not with her. Too many people are dead because of me already. She can't know, Dale. Swear to me you won't tell her!"

Dale glowered back at Marc.

"Swear it, Dale!"

"Fine. I won't say nothin'. But I think you're making a mistake," Dale grumbled.

"If it keeps her safe, it's worth it. Besides, she's stayed single this long. She'll still be available when this is over and I can explain it to her."

* * *

From her spot on the floor, Amy had glimpses of Dale and Marc talking as the two medics worked around her. She found their ministrations annoying. One was starting an IV while the other was bandaging her head. They were fussing like a couple of mother hens. What a lot of bother over a simple little scratch. The worst part was they kept blocking her view of Marc.

He and Dale seemed to be arguing about something. Dale was getting quite agitated. His face was flushed and he was waving his arms as he spoke. Marc, however, just stood scowling and listening to Dale, shaking his head at the same time. She wished she could hear what they were saying. Finally, the medics were done and helped her onto the stretcher.

They covered her with a blanket before starting to strap her down for transport to the hospital. Amy looked over towards Marc again and found his eyes locked on hers. A little jolt passed through her from the intensity of his gaze. The medics lifted the stretcher to its highest position and began wheeling her towards the door.

"Wait!" Marc called, pushing past Dale and striding towards them. "I need to take a statement from her." The medics stood waiting with barely concealed impatience until Marc growled, "Alone." Catching a glimpse of his expression, they shrank back and disappeared into the kitchen.

Marc waited until they were out of earshot then knelt closer to Amy. He started to reach towards her, then stopped and folded his arms across his chest instead.

Looking uncomfortable, he said, "I'm sorry, but I won't be able to go with you to the hospital. I have to finish up with this crime scene here then get back to my home base right away. We have to move quickly if we're going to get the rest of this gang. As soon as word gets out that these two are dead the rest will scatter."

"That's okay," she said, faking a smile. "I understand." She knew he'd be gone as soon as he remembered. She'd known it all along. She blinked furiously, trying, by sheer force of will, to keep the tears from welling up, but her vision blurred anyway.

She watched Marc glance furtively over his shoulder towards where Dale was busy directing the evidence gathering with two other officers, then off towards the two medics chatting in the kitchen. He turned back towards her for a moment, as if undecided. The next instant, Amy's eyes flew wide as his lips touched hers, softly, tenderly. He lingered only a moment before whispering in her ear, "Wait for me."

Standing abruptly, as if nothing had happened, Marc called out to the medics, "She's done now." In a low voice he added, "I'll keep in touch."

He turned away from her and didn't even watch as they wheeled her out of the house. He just stood there, back stiff and unyielding, watching the officers collect evidence. Amy willed herself not to cry as he disappeared from her line of sight. It was all too confusing. Five minutes ago he was holding her as if she was the most important thing in the world, and now he couldn't make the time to see her safe to the hospital. It all felt so eerily familiar somehow, her being taken off by ambulance, alone. At least this time she knew the love of her life wasn't going to come see her there. She wouldn't be lying in her room like an idiot, waiting for him to come through the door declaring his undying love. He had more important things to do. After all, he was an undercover agent with a life too dangerous to be tied down by a girlfriend.

"Twelve years alone, and I finally fall in love only to pick the wrong guy again," Amy muttered under her breath, wiping a tear off her face with the back of her hand.

Then he had to confound her even more with that kiss. How was she supposed to forget him with the memory of that kiss burned into her heart? And what was 'wait for me' supposed to mean? At least he said he'd keep in touch. Maybe, when he called, she'd be able to find out a little bit more. Who he was, and what, if anything, he wanted from her. Was that kiss just to say thanks for helping him out? Did he want to stay friends? Dare she hope for anything more? It would be good to talk. She found herself looking forward to his call.

The call never came.

Chapter Twenty-Eight

"Just tell me if she's okay." Marc tried to pitch his voice just loud enough to be heard over the phone without being overheard in the noisy pub.

"Why don't you ask her yourself?" was Dale's gravelly reply.

"Come on, Dale! You know I can't do that."

"Won't, you mean."

"Won't. Can't. Same diff. Is she?" Marc glanced around to make sure no one was listening.

"It's not and you know it," Dale grumbled. "She's well enough, I suppose. Clinic's doing well. She works too much and is looking a little skinny, if you ask me."

"Is she sick?" Marc asked anxiously.

"Nah. Just mopin' around with a face as long a mule's. You should stop by. Say hello. She did nurse you back to health after all. No one would think much of it if you did."

"I'll think about it," Marc hedged. "Thanks, Dale. Keep an eye on her for me."

"Always do."

Marc hung up the phone and leaned back against the wall staring at the ceiling. In the background, his fellow officers talked and laughed over their beers. Marc could join them if he wanted. They'd given him a hard time when he'd first switched from beer to cola but he hadn't backed down and they'd given up teasing him about it. He didn't really mind. They were good-natured about it. Still, it wasn't their company he wanted.

Amy haunted his every thought. There was nothing he wanted more than to do what Dale said. He longed to see Amy, hear her laugh, taste her lips once more, hold her close. But could he risk it? Someone had taken a couple of shots at him the first week he'd been back, but that gang member had been caught, and all had been quiet since. The court case was being rushed through, but there would still be several more months before he was finished testifying and no longer a threat. Could he risk it?

Marc wandered back out through the pub to the front entrance. He stared out the glass doors as a few random snowflakes drifted down from the night sky. A little gust of wind forced its way under the door, sending a shiver up his spine.

It was almost Christmas. Maybe he could just call it a social visit to repay her kindness. Would anyone buy that? He doubted it.

What if he left right now? It was only nine. He could be at her place by midnight if he didn't stop. They could talk a few hours. He could explain why he couldn't call or write, that he was trying to protect her. He could be gone before dawn and no one would know.

He chewed on it a few minutes, his heart beating faster at the thought of seeing her. Marc spun on his heel and went back into the bar to grab his coat.

"You leaving?" his buddy, Baker, called out.

"Going for a drive. Just need to clear my head." It was a good excuse. They'd all done the same at one time or another.

"It's cold out there. Stay."

Marc just waved him off with a grin and strode towards the door.

Baker yelled at his retreating back, "Well, if you're bent on leaving, at least try out the new remote starter you got with that pretty little black sports car the department gave you! No sense getting into a cold car if you don't have to!"

"Good idea!" Marc called back. He'd almost forgotten about that gizmo. The men's laughter followed him out into the parking lot as he fished the key fob out of his pocket. Might as well try the thing out, not that the car would warm up much in the ten seconds it would take him to walk to it. A gust of cold wind sliced through his jacket as he pointed the key fob and pressed the button. He took one stride as the car lights blinked, another stride as the engine turned over.

In an instant, Marc knew he had been wrong. Wrong to think it might be safe to see Amy. Wrong to believe things had settled. Wrong to let his guard down even for a second.

He barely had time to turn his back as his car exploded in a massive fireball of force which slammed into him, sending him flying back across the parking lot.

* * *

Amy stood on her sundeck, leaning on the railing in the warm spring sunshine as the breeze ruffled though her hair. It had been six and a half months since she had last seen Marc. Six and a half long, silent months, and his memory still burned in her heart.

After the shooting, she had spent a couple of days in the hospital while they ran a head CT and a few other tests to make sure she was okay, then she'd stayed at Candace's house for a few more weeks. First the police had to finish up their investigation, then the restoration company had to clean up the mess. It had taken weeks for all traces of the blood and carnage to be erased completely, but the end result was amazing. No one could tell from looking that anything unusual had ever happened in her home.

Below her, Amy could see Franz stalking a robin on the lawn. The cat was flattened to the ground, creeping slowly towards the bird, his tail twitching with suppressed excitement. Franz stopped and tucked his hindquarters in. He wiggled his butt, preparing to pounce.

"BAD CAT!" Amy yelled at the top of her voice. The robin exploded into the air, chirping in alarm, before Franz could leap. The cat sat up, looking miffed with his ears pointed out sideways. He sent a baleful look up towards Amy.

"Tough luck, fuzz-ball. No hunting birds while I'm around." She smiled for a moment, then sighed deeply.

It was time for her to get ready for work, but she couldn't help dawdling. She and Marc had spent so many warm fall nights out there on the deck, talking and laughing, it was almost like a little piece of him lingered there still. She was loath to leave.

She went upstairs to the bathroom sink with her cosmetic bag and started applying her eye makeup as her thoughts drifted back to Marc. It was hard to believe he had been gone for over six months. Everywhere she looked in the house there were little things to remind her of him. She'd still walk past his room and do a double-take because she thought she'd seen him reclining on the bed.

Sometimes she'd wake abruptly in the night and sit bolt upright, listening for him, only to hear nothing but Bella's soft snoring. Even in the clinic, there were little reminders everywhere, like the subtle dent in the wall where he had slammed David into it. She kept meaning to fix that, but never seemed to get around to it.

He had asked her to wait for him and she had. She'd waited for months and months but he never called. He never sent a text or email, not even a stupid Christmas card. She never really expected he would, but this stupid little part of her had kept clinging to hope saying 'maybe he will'. Silent tears welled within her eyes and she grabbed a tissue to wipe them away before her makeup smudged. Stupid! Should have used waterproof. She grabbed a different eyeliner and mascara.

There must be a reason, some explanation for his silence. She thought of his kiss, his whispered "wait for me…" It was driving her mad. She needed to let go, to get on with her life. But, what if… What if there was a good explanation for all of it? What if she gave up too soon?

Amy trudged down the stairs and went straight to the clinic, skipping breakfast for the fourth time that week. As she wandered into the office area, Candace flashed her a cheery grin.

"Check out the newspaper," she chirped. "Your old flame made the front page."

"My old flame?" Amy blurted, feeling a surge of excitement.

"Yeah. David's been convicted."

"Oh. Him," Amy replied, her voice dropping.

"Of course him. How many old flames have you had?" Candace asked, laughing.

Amy flushed slightly and hid her face by turning towards where the paper lay on the counter. She hadn't told anyone about her feelings for Marc. She didn't want the sympathy or the reminders of how similar this was to last time. After all, Marc hadn't even officially been her boyfriend. He'd wanted to be, before his memory returned, but then, after, he'd just disappeared.

Of course Dale kept bringing his name up. It was "Marc this," and "Marc that." Amy hung on every word, but had to pretend it was just a casual interest. How could she admit to Dale how deeply she missed Marc? She hadn't pined for David half this bad, and she'd known him far longer than she had Marc. Lately, even Dale had been silent. It was as if Marc had never existed.

Amy glanced at the banner half-heartedly. "Local Man Convicted in Statewide Drug Bust" it screamed. Her eyes drifted over the page. There was a big photo of David, too, but it was the other, smaller inset, that grabbed her eyes and wouldn't let go. Amy struggled to breathe as she clutched the counter, staring. Her hand slowly moved over and drew the paper closer.

There he was, Marc, looking gorgeous, as usual. He was laughing, happier than she'd ever seen him. He stood on the courthouse steps, in a tailored suit, with his arm wrapped around a tall, gorgeous woman with wavy dark hair that cascaded over her shoulders. He was looking straight into her eyes as she laughed up at him, the love between them unmistakable. The caption below just mentioned their names, Marcus and Tracy Taylor.

Amy stood rooted to the spot. There it was, the answer to the question she'd never had the nerve to ask. Marc's wife, right beside him on the front page of the paper. No wonder he hadn't called or written.

"Are you all right, Amy?" Candace sounded worried. "You've gone all white. You're not still hung up on David, are you?"

"N-no," Amy replied as her hand closed around the paper, scrunching it in her fist. "I, um.." She couldn't think straight. Couldn't form words. All she could do was walk to the shredder, and stuff the paper in.

"Hey! What are you doing? I haven't read that yet," Candace exclaimed, rushing over.

"Sorry," Amy said flatly, her face carefully composed. No one must know of her humiliation. She stiffened her spine and, with eyes just a little too shiny, smiled and said, "Here comes our first patient. Time to get to work."

* * *

Marc's car pulled into the gravel lot of Amy's clinic and came to a careful stop. He rolled his shoulders a couple times, trying to work the kinks out, and wiped his palms on his jeans. His heart was racing. He took a deep breath and let it out slowly. This was crazy. He could face down a whole courtroom full of gangsters and drug lords, but he was scared to death to talk to a pretty little blonde.

What if she didn't feel what he did? He thought she had, before. She had been afraid to kiss him because she had strong feelings for him, or at least that's what she claimed, but that was almost eight months ago. At least she still wasn't dating anyone. He'd been right about that. Dale had told him so. He only hoped she wouldn't be too angry with him once he had a chance to explain.

Technically, the case still wasn't finished in the courts, but his part was done now. He had testified and been cross-examined. No one could change that now. It was part of the court records. If anything were to happen to him now it would only make the gang look even guiltier, and they knew it. The members might be dumb as sticks, but the leaders weren't. He was finally free of the whole mess.

It was finally safe to see Amy again.

He grabbed the bouquet of roses and slipped out of the car. His hand hesitated for a moment on the doorknob as he steadied his nerves.

"Hello! Anybody home?" he called out into the silent clinic. It struck him as odd that it was so empty. His voice echoed softly back to him. He'd expected at least a patient or two to be there. Marc heard a noise around the corner and called hopefully, "Amy?"

A sweet-faced brunette with a pixie cut came around from the back room and said, "I'm sorry, but we're closed."

"Closed? I'm looking for Amy. Aren't you usually open Saturday mornings?" Something wasn't right.

"Usually," she replied cautiously, studying his face. "But Amy's not here."

"That's okay," Marc said, fighting off his disappointment. He pulled up a chair from the waiting area. "I'll wait. When do you expect her back?"

Candace approached closer, still scrutinizing him. "You look familiar," she puzzled. "Do I know you?"

"I don't think so," he answered evenly. "My name is Marc. Amy and I are… friends. And you must be Candace, right? Amy's mentioned you to me."

"That's right," she said, frowning slightly. "Though, I can't say Amy mentioned you at all. I still think I've seen you somewhere."

"I've been in the paper once or twice over the past few months. Maybe you saw me there."

Candace's eyes flew wide at the mention of the paper. "*You!*" she accused, pointing her finger. "You're the guy in the paper! You're behind all this!"

"What *this*? What's going on?" Marc didn't like the way this was starting to sound. The feeling of oddness was blossoming into full-blown anxiety.

"I don't know what's going on in her crazy little brain! She's been tight-lipped as a clam." Candace started pacing and gesturing wildly as she spoke. "I mean, she's been quiet and moody since before last Christmas, but she's always been a bit of a loner, so I didn't think much of it at the time. *Then* she saw that newspaper about six weeks ago. Something snapped. She went white as a sheet. Like, she just kinda shut down. The Amy I know wasn't there anymore!"

Marc's mind was racing. What could she have read that upset her so?

"Then," she continued, swinging back on him, "two weeks ago, she announces that she's leased the clinic out to another vet and she's leaving. She sent Bella into quarantine. She asked me to look after Franz! Now I gotta work with some new vet I don't even know! Because of you! What did you do to her?"

"Nothing! I haven't even spoken to her in months."
Maybe that was the problem right there, he thought angrily.
Why hadn't he listened to Dale? Why hadn't Dale warned
him? Marc sprang to his feet. He grabbed Candace by her
shoulders to stop her pacing. Pulling her to within inches of
his face, he repeated, "Where has she gone?"

"South Africa."

Chapter Twenty-Nine

Marc released her, and took a step back dropping his arms. "She... She went to Africa?" he repeated in astonishment.

"South Africa. She's gone to volunteer as a vet over there. She got a one-way ticket."

Marc dropped back into his chair.

Gone.

Not just gone for the day but gone to another continent. He stared across the room, seeing nothing. It felt as if his heart had just dropped out of his chest.

"Man, it's too bad you didn't show up a couple hours ago. Maybe you could have talked her out of it."

Marc's head snapped up. "What are you saying? Did she just leave? Just now?" He was on his feet and clutching her by the shoulders again. He had to force himself not to shake the answers out of her. "When did she leave? Where was she headed?"

"Sea-Tac Airport. About three hours ago. I'm not sure when the plane leaves, but there's a copy of her itinerary on the counter."

Candace stumbled back as Marc abruptly released her and whirled to grab the sheet of paper from the counter. There it was, her flight number and departure time. He glanced at his watch. Maybe. If there was no traffic. If all the lights were green. If God were with him.

"Thanks," he called over his shoulder as he dashed from the clinic.

"You'll never make it!" Candace called after him. "It's way too far!"

"Please, God, please..." he prayed as he stomped the gas and fish-tailed out of the parking lot.

Marc drove like a man possessed but it wasn't good enough. It was as if the universe had conspired against him and all his fervent praying useless. The traffic was horrible, road construction slowed him, and if there was a red light within a five mile radius, he hit it. By the time he reached the airport and parked, there were only minutes until take-off.

Marc raced through the airport, dodging travelers and luggage, running like a professional football player racing for the end zone.

He stopped only once, to check the display board for her gate number, and then was running again. People stared as he flew by, but he didn't care. He had to stop her from getting on that plane. He had to.

As he turned the corner into Gate 42, people milled everywhere. He dashed over to the flight attendant behind the desk.

"I have to speak to someone on United Flight 262. Can I go on? Just for a minute?" Marc pleaded breathlessly.

"I'm sorry sir, but that's not possible," she replied firmly.

"Please. It's important. Just for a moment?"

Her eyes, almost as dark brown as her skin, met his sympathetically. "I wish I could help you, sir, but..."

"Then help me. I have to talk to her."

She sighed and pointed out the window. "That's the plane you want, right there."

Marc's eyes followed her finger to the big silver plane, sunlight glinting off its bright blue tail fin, as it rose steadily upward through the afternoon sky.

* * *

Amy stared morosely out the window at the curving sloped roof of Dulles International Airport as her plane settled down onto the runway. Her mother's words still echoed in her mind.

"You're just running away again, you know. You'll never get anywhere that way."

Easy for her to say. She hadn't been dumped and humiliated by her fiancé. She hadn't waited alone for twelve years only to be dumped again. She wasn't stupid enough to make the same mistakes over and over. She didn't realize how deeply Amy had longed for Marc to come back, professing his love for her and a newfound faith in God. She didn't realize how completely impossible that dream had become now that Amy knew the truth.

Why? Why had he kissed her? Asked her to wait? Why not just tell her he was married? Why let her dream of more? Probably just keeping his options open, just like David would have done.

Amy grabbed her carry-on as the plane began to disembark. The words of an old Pink Floyd song from her college days floated through her mind. "I have become… Comfortably numb…"

She wished it were true, but she wasn't that lucky. She seemed to ache to the very core of her being. It took all her strength just to keep moving, keep functioning, pretend to be normal. Amy trudged down the gangway and into the terminal.

You should be in church praying instead of running off to Africa, her mother's words floated after her from across the country.

Hmph. A lot she knew. Amy had prayed. And prayed, and prayed, and prayed. She'd fasted and prayed.

Prayed 'til she was blue in the face, so to speak. What good had it done? Nothing. She was still single. Maybe she'd always be single. Didn't the Bible say some had the gift of being single? Some gift! If that was His *gift* God could keep it.

Amy swallowed past the lump in her throat and scanned the departures board for her next gate. Where was Ethiopian Flight 501? There.

She plodded on down the terminal until she arrived at the waiting area. She found a seat and plopped down. Only three and a half hours left to kill before her next flight. Good thing she'd brought a book.

Almost three hours later Amy still sat staring at the same page, mind wandering down paths of self-recrimination. Over the PA system, the steward announced pre-boarding for her flight. Amy closed her book and stuffed it in her bag. Who was she kidding? She wasn't reading it anyway. She leaned back and closed her eyes a moment.

"Amy!"

Her eyes flew open as her breath caught in her throat, but she didn't move. It couldn't be. Not here. Not now. But how could she mistake that voice? Slowly, she turned her head to look.

It was impossible.

There he was, striding purposefully towards her, pinning her to the spot with the sheer force of his gaze. Amy just stared, caught between the desire to run and hide before she could embarrass herself further, and the almost physical need to be in his presence just one more time. He looked tired and disheveled and entirely delicious. A five o'clock shadow darkened his jaw, and it looked as if he'd been running his hands through his hair again. Some small, random part of her brain noted with pleasure that he had lost all trace of the limp he'd had last time she saw him. It seemed so long ago now, like someone else's life.

She looked up into his face as he came to stand in front of her. Too late to run now. She forced herself to her feet.

"W-what are you doing here?" she managed in a hoarse whisper.

"That would seem fairly obvious, I'd think. I'm trying to catch up to you!" Marc answered, still breathing hard from racing through the airport.

"But, why?"

"Why?" Marc exhaled loudly. "Because I'm finished with that case now. My part is over. I came to see you, but you'd already left. Candace told me where to find you."

"B-but I left this morning. From Seattle. Why are you *here*?"

"When I missed your flight in Seattle, I booked myself on the next flight I could find heading to Washington. Amy, we need to talk. What are *you* doing here?"

"Well, I should be boarding my plane to Africa, not that it's any of your business! And you haven't answered my question. I don't care *how* you got here. I want to know *why*. Especially now, after all this time." She stood, arms crossed in front of her, as some of the color slowly returned to her face.

Mark suddenly looked unsure of himself, and swallowed noticeably before saying, "Because I thought we had something, Amy, an attraction between us. You felt it, too. I know you did." He reached out to touch her but she stepped back out of his reach.

"I'm sure there was some… purely physical attraction," Amy hedged, taking another step back, "but that was a long time ago."

"I know. I'm sorry, but I had to finish off this case first. I told you that. I'm here now, though."

"Now that I'm supposed to be getting on a plane to Africa? It's a little late, don't you think? Where were you six months ago?" As the shock of seeing him wore off, Amy's temper started to flare. Why couldn't he just let her crawl off to Africa to lick her wounds in obscurity?

"I'm sorry. I had a lot of loose ends to tie up with the case. These things take a long time. I asked you to wait. Amy, why didn't you wait for me?"

There was a note of hurt in his voice but she ignored it. She was too busy trying to hide the hurt in her own heart, and the only tool available to her was anger.

"Wait? I did wait. I waited and waited but you never called. No email or text. Nothing. Not even a lousy Christmas card! You said you'd keep in touch!"

"I did. I must have called Dale at least twice a week to see how you were doing. He told me everything you've been up to. He told me how you saved the mayor's dog after it was hit by a car. I heard about the filly you delivered at the racing stable. I even know Mrs. Dawson adopted two old dogs."

Amy's jaw dropped. "That's not keeping in touch. That's spying on me!" she flared indignantly.

"It's not like that…"

"Yeah? What's it like then? You remember your life, almost get me killed, and then you drop off the face of the planet."

At the mention of almost getting her killed, Marc flinched as if he'd been physically hit. She saw the guilt flood over him, and felt her resolve begin to waver. He had saved her life, too. It really wasn't his fault.

"I-I'm sorry. I didn't mean that. Look, I have to go. My plane is boarding."

Amy grabbed her bag and turned away from him. She'd better get away quickly, while she still had the will to do it.

Before she could take a step, Marc grabbed her by the arm and swung her back to face him. The guilt in his eyes was overshadowed by anger now as he met her glare. She'd seen that look before and knew it meant trouble.

"Don't be sorry," he growled. "You're right. I did almost get you killed. That's why I dropped off the face of the planet. To keep you safe!"

"Right. You stick with that story," she retorted sarcastically, trying to pull away. "I know what you've been up to."

Around them, a small circle of space had appeared as people backed away to give the illusion of privacy. They all sat or stood on the periphery, pretending to be otherwise occupied, as they listened in to the scene unfolding beside them. Marc glared around at them, then, with Amy still in hand, pushed past them and marched her to a quieter corner of the waiting area.

"So, you think you know what I've been up to, do you? You know they tried to shoot me a couple more times, then?" Marc said in a hoarse whisper. When her face paled visibly he continued, "Oh? Didn't know about that one?

What about the night I finally decided I had to see you? Good thing I used the remote car starter because I was still fifty feet away when the car exploded and pelted me with shrapnel! I spent five hours in the hospital waiting for the doc to dig little bits of car out of my backside. Thank God for leather jackets or it could have been worse. And then," he said, pausing for effect, "then they found my sister. She works for the D.A.'s office. They started sending threatening letters about what they'd do to her if I didn't change my testimony. I had to have her put in protective custody. Do you have any idea what that's like? Knowing you could be the reason someone you love dies?" His voice got louder with every statement.

"I-I'm sorry. I had no idea," Amy said defensively.

"You have no idea about a lot of things, Amy! Those two I killed were just the first few pebbles of a full-blown avalanche. What do you think would have happened to you if the gang found out how much I love you? You'd be a target…"

"You don't love me," she interrupted, backing away from him.

He couldn't possibly love her. She'd seen him with his wife. Seen the love in his eyes for her. She was so beautiful. He couldn't have left her for someone like Amy. And if he had? It would only be a matter of time before he dumped Amy for someone better. No. She refused to believe it.

"I do!" He reached out to touch her cheek but dropped his hand again as she leaned back away from him.

"That's why I had to stay away from you. To keep you safe. I almost got you killed once. I couldn't live with myself if something happened to you because of me. I already carry enough guilt over my parents' deaths." His voice had dropped low again as he pleaded for her to understand.

"You said they died in a car accident," she countered warily.

"They did, but it was my fault." He paused, appearing unwilling to continue, but as she stood there, unwavering, he forced the words out. "I was seventeen, a senior in high school. I was supposed to be studying but I wanted some cola to stay awake. My mother said she'd get some in the morning but that wasn't good enough for me. Oh, no. I had to have it right away. How could I study without cola?" he continued, sounding full of self-loathing. "So my dad offered to go.

"'Good', I thought. I wanted what I wanted, when I wanted it. Mom offered to go with him. That's the way they were, always together." He paused and looked away. His voice dropped as he spoke again. "That's the last time I saw them alive. A drunk driver hit them. They died instantly. I had to identify their bodies. Their eyes were still open when I saw them..."

"Marc, I'm so sorry," Amy breathed. Her heart broke for the pain she saw in his face. "But that wasn't your fault. It was the drunk's fault. Surely you see that?"

"If I hadn't been so selfish," he said, swinging back towards her, "If I had only put their welfare first, they'd still be alive." He reached out and took her by the shoulders. Pulling her closer to him, he pleaded, "Can you understand why I had to stay away? I couldn't let my selfish desires put you in danger again. Amy, I love you. I was trying to protect you."

Amy shook her head as she pulled back from him. It took all her will to do it. The deepest desire of her heart was to pull him close, soothe his pain and tell him she loved him, too. She fought back tears as she fought her own instincts. She longed to believe him, swallow it, hook, line, and sinker, but the specter of Tracy loomed in front of her.

"I'm sorry for what you've been through. I'm flattered you feel that way, but we were only ever just friends," she lied. "I'm sorry if you got the wrong impression. I never felt that way about you…" Her voice faltered at the look on his face.

Marc straightened his spine, seeming to visibly pull a blank mask on like before, when he was trying to shield himself. A little muscle in his jaw twitched, and she knew his emotions were barely in check.

"So, you feel nothing? Is that what you're telling me?" His voice was ominously quiet.

"I - I have to go…" she faltered. I think they're calling my name." Amy fumbled with her bag and turned to leave.

She took one step before Marc grabbed her arm, swung her around and pulled her into his embrace. His mouth came down on her lips with dizzying intensity. When he'd kissed her before, it had been sweet, gentle, and tender, coaxing her to respond. This time it was fiery and passionate, demanding a response, accepting no less than her full surrender. Amy couldn't fight it. She melted into his arms, opening her mouth to his and returning his kiss with full abandon even as the tears filled her eyes.

He released her suddenly, stepping back with obvious difficulty as he brought himself under control. "I thought you said you felt nothing," he rasped softly as he stood blocking her escape route.

Amy had stumbled back as he released her, and stood with her back to the wall and her hand pressed to her mouth. Tears spilled down her cheeks as she sobbed, "Why are you doing this? Why can't you just let me go?"

"Because God brought us together for a reason, Amy. You taught me that. We're meant to be together, you and I." He didn't try to touch her, yet she shivered in his presence.

"I said God wanted me to save you, not that we were meant to be together forever," she countered. "Besides, you're not even a believer. Where do you get off lecturing me about faith?"

"But I *am* a believer," he replied quietly, his eyes piercing hers. "Remember? I told you I'd prayed."

"It takes more than one prayer of desperation to make you a true believer."

"I know." His voice was deceptively calm. "You have to confess your faults, which I did. You have to change your attitude about God, see Him as someone who loves you and wants to help you rather than some mindless entity that doesn't care or just wants to punish you. You have to love Him back. I've done that, Amy. I've dropped some bad habits and picked up a few better ones. Isn't that what you wanted? Why are you still resisting this?" He reached out and gently brushed a tear from her cheek, but she thrust his hand away.

"You can't just do all that stuff to impress me, you know. That doesn't count."

"I didn't do it for you. I did it for me." His voice hardened, like steel. "I learned to trust you, and to trust in the God you believed in. Why aren't you trusting Him now? Why are you running away from us?"

"I know! Okay?" Her voice rose shrilly as she unleashed all her pain and anger on him. "I know about Tracy! Why are you saying all these things to me when you have her? You shouldn't even be here. What is this? Some sort of extra booty on the side? Or did you dump her, you lying, cheating, slimy, weasel-faced..." Amy's voice trailed off as she saw the open-mouthed, confused look on Marc's face. She also noted that half the airport seemed to be staring at them.

"*What* are you talking about?" he asked, looking bewildered.

"Your wife!"

Chapter Thirty

"My what!"

"Your wife. Tracy Taylor. I saw your picture in the paper. Don't try to deny it," she raged quietly. "I saw the way you looked at each other. I'm not stupid."

"Tracy?" he asked again, incredulously.

"I saw you together in the paper. Did you honestly believe I wouldn't find out?"

Amy's tirade stopped abruptly. Marc had dropped into a chair with a big, ridiculous grin on his face and was actually laughing. He looked positively joyful. Amy stared at him in confusion.

"Is that what this is all about?" He grinned. "Sweetheart, Tracy is my sister. She's my younger, unmarried sister."

Amy stood still as a statue, staring at him dumbfounded. "Your sister?" she repeated stupidly.

"Yes," he said, pulling her down to sit beside him.

Her legs felt like jello and she collapsed into the seat beside him with no protest. His sister. She was his sister. Amy could see the woman in her mind's eye. Tall. Deep blue eyes. Long dark brown hair in a riot of curls.

Impossibly gorgeous. Of course she was his sister. She was a female version of Marc!

"I know the picture you mean," Marc continued. "It was taken the day I finished testifying and Tracy was allowed out of protective custody and back to work at the courts. We were pretty happy to see each other." Marc was still grinning like a Cheshire cat. "Why did you think she was my wife? The article was pretty clear about who she was."

Amy's face flamed as she looked down at her hands. "I didn't actually read the article," she mumbled.

"You didn't?" Marc prodded.

"No. I, um, kinda shoved it in the shredder." She fidgeted uncomfortably under his amused gaze. "I saw the names, and the way you were looking at each other and…"

"You assumed she was the mythical wife you thought I must have hidden somewhere," he finished for her, looking far too pleased with himself. "You were jealous! You do care!"

Amy nodded mutely. Her lip trembled as she looked up to meet his eyes as her own brimmed with unshed tears. "I care a lot," she said, barely above a whisper. "I'd hoped beyond hope that when your memory came back there might be some way we could be together, that'd you'd still like me after you remembered your real life. Then you got your memory back, and just disappeared from my life, like you'd never been there. You left such an empty hole, Marc. I kept hoping. Waiting. I told myself there had to be an explanation.

"Then I saw the picture, and there she was, the reason why you never called. I guess it was easier to believe you had a wife who loved you, than to think you just couldn't be bothered with me..."

"Amy, there's never been anyone but you. In the years after my parents' deaths, I was too busy trying to finish school, look after my baby sister, and just survive, to have time for dating. I joined the police force first, to help put Tracy through university. Then I made the move to the DEA. You can imagine the type of women I met while undercover. Not exactly anyone I'd want to bring home. And then there you were." He reached out and gently brushed a tendril of hair off her cheek.

"From the moment I woke up in your home, you completely captivated me. Somehow I knew I had something with you that I'd never had before, even when I couldn't remember anything else. The hardest thing I've ever done, was let that ambulance drive away with you inside. No, maybe staying away afterwards was harder. I thought of you every day, prayed for you, drove Dale crazy with endless phone calls checking up on you." He chuckled softly, and then sobered as he looked directly into her eyes. "I love you, Amy, with all my heart. I never want us to be apart again. Never. If you won't come back to Washington with me, then I guess I'm going to South Africa."

"Really? You'd do that?" Amy could barely believe her ears. She searched his face for a trace of doubt, but found none. After so many months of waiting, and weeks of believing him married, to finally hear the words she'd longed for, was almost too much to take in. Love welled within her, so overwhelming she didn't know whether to laugh or cry. Finally, she did both, as she blurted, "I love you, too, Marc. So much!"

Marc's answering grin seemed a little relieved as he stood and pulled her up to face him. He cupped her face in his hands, kissed her gently on the lips, lingering a moment, sending deliciously, tingly shivers down her spine, then dropped to one knee in front of her. Amy felt her eyes grow wide as he kissed her hand and said, "Amy Scott, would you do me the honor of becoming the real Mrs. Taylor? Will you marry me?"

She couldn't speak, but she hoped her huge grin and wildly nodding head spoke for her. With a whoop of joy Marc stood and swept her up in his embrace, twirling her around as he did so. They were both laughing so hard it took a moment for them to notice that everyone else in the waiting area was cheering and clapping, too.

Amy felt her face redden as Marc took a bow before their audience. Standing again, he pulled her close and whispered, "I'm sorry, darling, but I think I made you miss your plane." He indicated out the window where Ethiopian Flight 501 was taxiing down the runway.

"Oh no!" Amy cried as she ran to the window, dismayed.

"What? You still want to go?" Marc asked, anxiously.

Amy turned back to him with a tender but worried smile. "No. But Bella's on the plane. She's gone to Africa without me!"

"Oh." Marc paused a moment. "You know, Africa would make an amazing honeymoon destination. We could get married there. Bella could be your bridesmaid," he said, amusement dancing in his eyes.

Amy considered a moment, then cracked a smile and said, "You're on, as long as you're the one who explains to my mother why she wasn't invited."

Marc wrapped his arm around her shoulders as they started down the hall, back towards the booking counters. "Deal. Now we just have to change your ticket and get one for me."

"Marc?" Amy asked, after walking awhile. "What do we do when we get back?"

"What do we do about what?"

"Well. I've leased out the clinic, but there's probably enough work to keep two vets busy. What about you, though? I don't want to have you disappear undercover for months at a time. I'd miss you, and I'd probably worry myself to death."

"No problem. I'll quit."

"Really? Just like that?"

He smiled down at her. "Yes. Just like that. It's not the life for a married man. Some guys do it, but their marriages suffer for it. I don't want that. Besides, I was getting tired of the lifestyle anyway."

"But what will you do instead? I saw you prowling around my house like a caged bear. You need to keep busy somehow."

"Well… there's a certain sheriff in town who wants to retire."

"Dale?"

"Yes, Dale. He's said that if I'd like to throw my hat in the ring, he and the other deputies will back me. What do you think? Want to be a small town sheriff's wife?"

Amy beamed up at him. "I'd *love* to be a small town sheriff's wife… as long as he's you!"

The End

Acknowledgements

There are so many people to thank for their input and assistance in making this book a reality.

Thank you to Brenda Sinclair, Alyssa Linn Palmer, Victoria Chatham, and Pamela Yaye for their editorial suggestions. You ladies are amazing.

Thank you to Beth Ross, Sherry MacDonald, and Roberta Jorgensen for their feedback on this story in its early stages.

Thank you to my cousin, Dr. Sharon Bruce DVM, for her suggestions regarding Amy's veterinarian clinic and activities.

A special thank you to the very talented Su Kopil from Earthy Charms Designs for crafting another beautiful cover for me. I absolutely adore it. Please check out her website at www.earthlycharms.com to view her designs.

Thank you to Ted Williams for the most precise and detailed line editing. Even though I nearly pulled my hair out when you advised me there was a problem with the layout of Amy's house/clinic, your suggestions have made the story better. Thank you!

And finally, thank you to my wonderful family for their patience and support as I wrote this novel. Love you all!

About The Author

Ellen Jorgy lives in Central Alberta with her husband, Bob, and two children, on a ten acre property with a menagerie of creatures both large and small. She works by day as a Medical Ultrasound Technologist, and by night as an unpaid taxi driver for her children. Somewhere in the midst of all that she finds time to write.

Never Alone is her second published work of fiction.

You can find Ellen at:

Website: *www.ellenjorgy.com*

Facebook @ellenjorg2

29838693R00184